SURVIVOR TURNED SOLDIER

Reardon felt the tug of memory—the night the aliens hit his camp. The street in front of him was filled with aliens. Hundreds of them, pouring into the center of the city, running and firing. Reardon aimed a shot at the center of the mass and saw a creature tumble to the street. Reardon fired again—missed, but there were so many aliens attacking that he hit another. He swung his laser in a wide arc. Four aliens went down. Suddenly he was lost in a vacuum where there was no one but him and the aliens. Aim, fire, aim, fire, aim, fire. The enemy soldiers fell. . . .

Ace Books by Kevin Randle

Jefferson's War Series

THE GALACTIC SILVER STAR
THE PRICE OF COMMAND

THE LOST COLONY
(coming in March 1991)

JEFFERSON'S WAR
THE PRICE OF COMMAND
KEVIN RANDLE

ACE BOOKS, NEW YORK

This book is an Ace original edition,
and has never been previously published.

THE PRICE OF COMMAND

An Ace Book / published by arrangement with
the author

PRINTING HISTORY
Ace edition / December 1990

ISBN: 0-441-38438-2

Ace Books are published by The Berkley Publishing Group,
200 Madison Avenue, New York, New York 10016.
The name "ACE" and the "A" logo
are trademarks belonging to Charter Communications, Inc.

PRINTED IN THE UNITED STATES OF AMERICA

10 9 8 7 6 5 4 3 2 1

THE PRICE OF COMMAND

1

THE STOCKADE MIGHT have been something out of the Old West on Earth except that the logs had all been machined to fit together perfectly and had been sharpened to a razor point by laser. The palisade was fourteen feet high with cameras mounted along it in place of guard towers, and covered almost three hectares. Inside were buildings of wood and stone, built by robots designed for construction, a generating station that used solar and geothermal springs for sources of power, and two hundred and thirty men, women, and children who had spent four years in space to arrive on the planet where they were promised a chance to start a new life. There were worlds to be conquered, resources to be tapped, and fortunes to be made. It was the dream that had dragged men and women across continents and oceans and now through space.

They had arrived only six months earlier, but even before the last of their shuttles had touched down, the stockade was up and the electronic surveillance was in place. They had moved into the temporary central dormitories, one for the men, one for the women, and one for families within hours of landing. Then the shuttles had roared back into space leaving them with only a radio link with Earth. That hadn't mattered because the few natives hadn't cared when the Earth people landed, as the planet was virtually uninhabited. There were plenty of wide-open spaces for those who wanted to claim them.

The leader of the expedition, Major Lucas P. Reardon, was pleased with the progress. They had planted Earth crops, seen them prosper in the rich, alien soil, had opened up trade with the natives, and had established themselves in the sun-bleached valley with its mild climate. It seemed that the recruiting posters, the propaganda, were all true.

Reardon walked across the compound and looked up into the alien night sky. There was a band of brightness across the zenith, the stars of galactic center blazing. A single, small moon was hanging low, looking slightly greenish. He stopped and watched the high clouds drift by. If there was one thing he missed about Earth, it was the dark nights. The very dark nights when it was impossible to see more than two feet. Here, even with the moon gone, the stars were bright enough to cast shadows.

He moved toward the security post. The one man on guard duty, watching the monitors, turned and looked at Reardon. He was a small man with jet-black hair and thin, sharp features. He was sitting in front of a bank of color monitors set into a plastic desk with a sloped rear. Near his right hand were control buttons, switches, and small joysticks that allowed him to direct the laser fire if the targeting computer missed anything. It was a defense for the entire compound, directed by one man with the help of the defensive computer.

"It's been real quiet, Luke. Real quiet."

Reardon pulled a chair around and sat down in it. He glanced at the screens arrayed in front of Stephen Garnett. Nothing showed on any of them.

"When's Caleb take over for you?"

"An hour or so." Garnett stretched, his arms high over his head. He groaned out loud and then seemed to collapse. "Wish we had some real coffee."

"I wish I had a Coke," said Reardon.

There was movement on one of the monitors and Garnett turned toward it. He adjusted the brightness and the contrast, trying to see better. Garnett tapped the glass of the screen.

"What is it?" asked Reardon.

Peering closer, Garnett shrugged. "Looks like a migration of animals."

"Shouldn't be time for a migration."

"How would we know? We've only been here for a few months. There's no way for us to be sure."

"Except that it seems to be the middle of summer here. Animals don't migrate in the middle of summer."

"That's on Earth. Here. Who knows?"

Reardon ignored that, stood, and stepped closer to the screen. The light amplification system they used gave the whole landscape a greenish, nightmarish cast. Everything was in shades of green from a bright, sickly yellow-green to a dark charcoallike color.

"I don't . . ."

"There," said Garnett. "Right there."

"Yeah. Sort of a mass like syrup on a table."

Garnett reached up toward the controls of the laser system but didn't touch them. It was set on automatic and if anything moved into the perimeter that met certain computer parameters, the lasers would open fire. Garnett turned and looked into Reardon's eyes.

"Let's see what we have first," he said.

The creatures kept coming, moving slowly, almost as if stalking the compound. Reardon wished that he could see what the creatures were. They seemed to be moving on all fours and were about the size of a big dog. But there was something about their movement. Not the innocent running of a pack, or the slow motion of them in migration. They seemed to be moving in on an unsuspecting prey.

"Well?" asked Garnett.

"Leave the defenses in place."

"Could be a bunch of animals."

"Then no harm done," said Reardon.

Garnett shrugged again and rocked back in his chair. He reached to the right for his cup of simulated coffee. They brewed it from local beans but the taste and texture weren't quite right. It was a little more bitter than the worst coffee ever brewed on Earth, and it didn't seem to contain any caffeine so that it wasn't the early morning help that coffee should be.

The creatures slipped into a shallow ditch and fanned out,

almost disappearing. Reardon sat up straighter and waited for them to reappear. He reached toward the button that would illuminate the outside perimeter.

Then, almost as if a command had been given, the creatures came boiling up, out of the ditch, running toward the stockade. When they were three hundred yards from the base of the logs, the defensive perimeter opened fire. Green flashes of brightness on the screen that left lingering images.

Creatures were hit, falling, stumbling, and rolling. There was no sound from them and no return fire. They kept coming, as if they didn't understand what was happening to them. As if they had no intelligence.

"Luke?"

More of the lasers were firing. The crisscrossing of the beams filled the screen, obscuring the targets. Bright, pencil-thin lines that looked like random bars thrown over the monitor. They flared and flashed and then disappeared as the attackers vanished.

"Cut it off," said Reardon.

Garnett punched a sequence on a number pad and the lasers stopped targeting. "You want the perimeter lights?"

"Not now," said Reardon. "Too much of a drain on the electrical system."

"Yeah," said Garnett. "Sure wouldn't want anyone to have to sleep without air-conditioning."

They watched the monitors, heads swiveling from one to the next, but the creatures, the enemy, whatever it had been, didn't reappear. The screens were blank except for the lumps that were the bodies of the things killed.

Garnett leaned forward and froze the view on one of the dead. He studied it carefully, moving around in his chair as if that could change his view of the creature. He tapped the screen finally and asked, "That one of the natives?"

"Can't tell," said Reardon. "We'll go out tomorrow and take a good look. We'll know then."

They sat quietly for a moment, letting the computer sequence its way through the various cameras showing different views around the camp. Nothing was moving now. Nothing was forming for an attack.

Reardon stood up and turned toward the door. He studied it

for a moment and then said, "If anything else develops, you let me know."

"Sure."

As Reardon moved to the door, the siren went off. A piercing wail that scared him. Reardon whirled and stared at the monitors, but they had gone blank.

"What the hell?"

Garnett was on his feet, leaning over, punching buttons. "I don't know. The wall is breached."

"What do you mean breached?"

"Something's coming through!"

Reardon didn't wait for anything more. He hit the button that would initiate an automatic emergency broadcast. There would be time later to retract it. If it needed to be retracted.

"Arm the lasers."

Garnett moved to do it, but by then it was too late.

2

THE GOLDEN GLOW of the city seen from the top floor of the spaceport terminal was deceiving. It was a warm, inviting glow, making the city look like something from the ancient fables. Streets and buildings and statues made from solid gold.

But that was the city seen through the thick glass of the windows, with the sun high overhead. When they finally got out into it, they would realize that it was a layer of thick pollution, hanging stagnant, threatening to choke everything in it. There was nothing warm and inviting about it. It was a cruel joke played by nature.

"How long has it been since you've been on Earth?" asked Victoria Torrence. She was only five seven, had brown hair and blue eyes. Her features were sharp, almost severe, but that was from living on army food for the last six months. After two weeks on Earth, eating the variety of starchy foods available, her face would soften slightly although her chin would still be pointed and her face still narrow.

David Jefferson glanced at her and shrugged. "Couple of years, give or take a month or two."

Jefferson was young to have been given the command of a combat regiment, but then he'd been in the middle of a war. That sometimes propelled people high quickly. George Custer, by being in the right place at the right time and by knowing no fear, had risen to the rank of major general within a couple of years of graduating from West Point. Jefferson, by being in the right place and by being surrounded by brave people, had accomplished almost the same thing.

Torrence tapped the glass. "I suppose we'd better get out there."

"You have plans?" asked Jefferson.

"I'm going to meet some of the other officers for lunch at the Royale Supreme and then we're going to head home on leave."

"Who all's going to be there?"

"Sinclair, Lynn, and I think Carter. Maybe one or two others. Depends on the assignments and who caught the morning moon shuttle and who didn't."

Jefferson glanced at his watch and knew that it was wrong. He'd set it while in orbit, but set it to ship time and not landing time. From the position of the sun he assumed that it was midmorning.

There was a bonging behind them and a feminine voice announced the arrival of the London–New York–Chicago shuttle. It would be on the ground for five minutes.

"I suppose I'd better get moving," said Jefferson.

Torrence reached out and touched him on the sleeve. "You are welcome to join us for lunch."

He turned and looked into her eyes and knew that he wasn't welcome. He didn't know whether it was because of what had happened during the last six months or if it was because he was the regimental commander. All he knew was that he wasn't welcome to join them for lunch no matter what Torrence said. "No. I'll pass on it."

She looked relieved but said, "If you're sure."

"Go," said Jefferson.

She nodded and said, "Back here in seventy-two hours." And then she ran off, joining the line of people waiting for a space in the tube.

Jefferson turned back toward the window and watched the traffic just outside. Cabs taking on passengers, the baggage loaded into the rear of them. There were only a few pedestrians. It was hard to see across the pavement and out into the open field that surrounded the port facilities.

Finally he walked away from the window, shouldering his way through the crowd. They were mostly military in a variety of uniforms from each branch of the service. There were civilians sprinkled in, mostly men. Jefferson tried to ignore them. Rather than fight the crowd, he drifted along with it, trying not to hear anything they said. Many of them smelled, the result of limited space on the shuttles that contained no bathing facilities. That was a luxury that no one could afford. Why waste the space and the payload for something as superfluous as water for bathing.

He reached the front of the port. It was a series of double doors that worked the same way as airlocks. It was designed to keep the fresh, recycled air in the building and the polluted, particle-laden air outside. Most of those coming in removed the filters they wore as soon as it was safe to do so.

Jefferson made his way through the doors and found himself on the sheltered sidewalk outside the port. He took a single breath. The air tasted of dirt and gas and oil. It was slimy and foul and he began to cough. He raised a hand for a taxi, and as soon as one appeared he dived into the back, slamming the door behind him.

"Gotta watch that, Gov. It'll do ya in."

Jefferson, his eyes watering, tried to get his breath. He nodded and pointed, but couldn't say anything for a moment.

"Take ya time, Gov."

Torrence rode the tube in silence, trying to ignore those around her and the lousy, almost-subliminal music that was playing over the hidden speakers. She sat there, eyes closed, and tried not to feel the motion. It wasn't the same as space where the lack of gravity made the constant motion impossible to feel. Here she could feel the acceleration and the deceleration and every one of the bumps as they were propelled along the corridor. All that was making her slightly sick to her stomach.

They slowed and stopped and the terminal name glowed bright above her head, seeming to hang in the middle of the air. When the doors popped open, Torrence exited and found herself in an underground station looking up a gentle slope that was brightly lighted. With dozens of others, she walked up as the corridor narrowed. There was a band of lights at the apex of the tunnel. Along the walls were posters selling everything from toilet paper to the joys of off-world exploration. There were ads for new holo movies and for safe sex and abstinence. Ads for air filters or for the reforestation of the Midwest and for the Fund to Restore the Brazilian Rain Forest. Everyone with a product or a cause had a poster. Torrence tried to ignore them, but she had been off Earth for nearly five years and the ads fascinated her.

She reached the top of the slope and the tunnel seemed to open up into a gymnasium-sized room filled with thousands of people. Forty feet above them were windows that showed the dirty yellow glow of the smog. No blue sky, no clouds, nothing. Just the smog hanging there.

She pushed her way through the masses, toward the corridor that led up into the lobby of the hotel, and then walked across the lobby. Once it might have been elegant and grand, but now it was shabby, filled with furniture that had seen better days. Hundreds of people with nowhere else to go had camped out in the lobby, sleeping or eating or just sitting, staring at nothing and watching nothing.

Even the narrow hallway that led to the restaurant was crowded with those who had taken up residence there. The odor of unwashed bodies and an open sewer hung in the air like the smog outside. Even the confines of the smallest of the fleet's ships had never smelled as bad as that hallway with its peeling paint and dirt-smeared walls.

She came to the door to the restaurant. Once it had been a fine door of carved wood with an oval window. Now there was plywood instead of glass and there were steel bars reinforcing the wood. Two burly men, each holding an ax handle, stood guard. They said nothing as she approached, just smiled and opened the door for her.

As she entered, she saw her friends sitting at a large round table stuck in the back. Carter half stood and waved and then dropped back into his seat as she started moving toward them.

Torrence dropped into the chair that had been left vacant for her. She looked at the food spread on the table and then picked up her glass, drinking the foul-tasting water. Even the bit of lemon floating in it failed to disguise the taste.

"I told you she wouldn't bring him," said Carter. He was the regimental S-2, the intelligence officer. He was a tall, thin man with black hair and pasty white skin. His eyebrows looked like a woolly caterpillar had crawled across his face and taken up residence.

"She asked though," said Sinclair. "I'll bet she asked." Sinclair was nearly as tall as Carter and was skinny. Like Carter, she had jet-black hair. There the resemblance ended. Sinclair had cold, steel-grey eyes.

Torrence nodded. "I asked him but he refused to come."

"Figures," said Jason Lynn. "Just like the asshole." Lynn was the youngest of the officers there. He was fair-haired and fair-skinned and was stocky, unlike most of the other space travelers. He had been with the battalion only a few months before Jefferson had joined it, and he resented Jefferson more than the others.

Torrence glanced at the young man, just barely out of his teens, and said, "The man is damned if he does and damned if he doesn't. Sinclair doesn't want him here and apparently you do."

"That's not what I said."

"It's the same thing," said Torrence. "You're pissed because he didn't come along. I know why he didn't. He figured his presence would ruin our fun."

"And he'd be right about that," said Sinclair.

"Shit," said Torrence. She grabbed her water and drank, pretending that it was fresh and sweet. "Have any of you ordered?"

"We were waiting for you," said Carter.

A waiter appeared then. He was dressed in black pants and a white shirt with a small, black bow tie. At one time the costume might have been elegant, but now it looked out of place, out of date, and shabby.

"Is there a Major Torrence here?"

"I'm Torrence."

"We have a call for you in the manager's office. If you'll follow me."

She stood up and mumbled, "I wonder what asshole got arrested this time."

Sinclair lifted her glass that didn't contain water. "Have fun, Major. We'll wait right here for you."

Torrence followed the waiter through the dining room, winding his way among the tables and then down a short corridor. He stopped outside a door, tapped on it, and then opened it. "In there," he said.

Torrence entered. It was a tiny room, reminiscent of those on the ship. A single desk was set so that anyone sitting behind it would be facing the door. A chair for the visitor was pushed into a corner. On the desk was a vid-phone. Torrence spun it around and said, "Yes?" She was looking at the head and shoulders of another officer.

"I have to advise you that your leave has been canceled and the recall is immediate. You are to return to the shuttle port for lift-off in three hours."

"But . . ."

"Are there any others with you?"

"Major Sinclair and Captains Carter and Lynn."

The head bowed and then looked up. "Do you know the location of Colonel Jefferson?"

"Negative."

"Three hours," said the officer and the screen went dark.

Jefferson didn't bother watching the traffic on the ride downtown. He sat in the back of the cab, separated from the driver by a bulletproof screen. The side windows were covered with a reflective coating making it difficult to see out and impossible to see in. Jefferson didn't care.

They arrived downtown and pulled to a curb. Through the driver's window, Jefferson saw the masses of people circulating with the relentlessness of a river's current. Jefferson tried to open the door and found it locked with no way for him to unlock it.

A slot opened in the bulletproof window between him and the driver. A tinny voice said, "That's a hunnert and twenny-five even."

"What?"

"Twenny-one miles. A hunnert and twenny-five. In the slot."

Jefferson pulled out a handful of bills and dropped them into the tray.

"Tip?"

Jefferson added a five and then pushed the slot closed. The locks snapped and he opened the door. The smog rolled in, filling the rear of the cab with its stench. Jefferson coughed once and then put his hand in front of his face.

"Shoulda sprung for a mask, Gov."

Jefferson slammed the door and turned to face the blank wall of the building. Nearly everyone in the crowd wore some kind of filter whether it was miniature nose filters that cost two hundred a pair or cheap cloth and plastic masks that were stained by the normal breathing of the owners.

Jefferson staggered to the door of the building and pushed it open. He found himself standing, facing another set of doors while filters tried to scrub the air. He moved forward, opened the next set of doors, and stepped into the main floor lobby of a hotel. The door snapped shut behind him but he could still taste the air. The door entry lock didn't work very well.

He moved toward the desk, stepping over the bodies of the people who lived in the lobby. The bored clerk watched and moved toward him when he got to the desk.

"Help you?"

"You have a room booked under the name of Jefferson?"

The man turned toward a card index, flipped through them, and asked, "David?"

"Yeah." Jefferson looked at the cobweb-covered computer with its broken screen and knew why they had slipped into the old-fashioned way.

"Your wife is waiting up in room five-oh-nine."

"A key?"

"You joke."

Jefferson shrugged and turned away from the desk. Before he could move, the clerk warned him: "Elevator's broke."

Jefferson waved a hand once and then picked his way through the lobby trying to avoid stepping on anyone or in anything. He found the door to the stairs. It was hanging by one hinge and on the other side he found more of the same. People staked out steps, one person to a step, and they weren't inclined to clear a path upward. Jefferson leaned over one person, who was lying on his side snoring, and grabbed the railing, lifting himself up and over. He climbed to the fifth floor that way, only stepping on two feet and one hand and kicking one woman in the head.

He opened the door and stepped into the hallway there, but things didn't improve. It was still hot and the air was heavy with the odor of hundreds of people. There were some lights and one broken chair. Jefferson worked his way along the hall until he found room five-oh-nine. When he tried the door, it was locked from the inside, so he knocked.

"Wait." Then the voice was closer. "Who is it?"

"Me."

"Wait." There was a rattling of a chain and then the snap of a lock. The door opened.

Jefferson pushed his way in, thinking that it would be cooler, cleaner, fresher inside, but it wasn't. The room was as shabby as the rest of the hotel. There was a bed with a paper-thin mattress and there was a grime-streaked window on the other side of it. There was a chair that had seen better days and a television that had a cracked screen.

"Hi," said the woman.

Jefferson turned and faced her. She'd changed from her uniform. She stood there wearing a civilian dress that was cut so that it concealed her body. There was a pointed tail in the front that reached down toward her ankles. The side was slit to the knee. The collar was buttoned to her throat and the whole thing ballooned out from the shoulders to be gathered at the waist.

"Courtney," said Jefferson.

"Colonel."

Jefferson laughed at that. He moved toward the chair and sat down. He looked up at her and thought of her momentarily as First Lieutenant Norris. A very young woman with bright blue eyes and long brown hair that hung down her back now that she was out of uniform.

"This room is costing four hundred and twelve dollars," she said.

"Christ."

"It's private. We have it until nine o'clock tomorrow and no one has the right to enter it."

Now Jefferson shook his head. "It was getting bad when I left Earth, but nothing like this."

"I know," said Norris.

"You'd think that someone would have made a right move sometime in the last couple of years."

"Makes the ship, even with its crowded quarters, seem luxurious."

"Hell, we don't even have crowding like this on the ship. People jammed in everywhere, on top of everyone."

Norris didn't want to talk about the ship or the living conditions on it. Instead, she turned once like a fashion model in the latest, most expensive dress ever created, and asked, "You like?"

"It's pretty."

"I bought it before we left he station in the shuttle. Had a shop there by the main access corridor."

"You didn't have to," said Jefferson. His voice was lifeless.

She looked at him. "You feeling okay?"

Now he stood and moved to the window but the smog kept him from seeing down into the street. It was a yellow cloud streaked with black and grey below him and above him. There was the hint of another building in the distance but no evidence that anything lived on the planet.

"I'm fine," he said. Then, looking at her, he added, "You know that we have to keep this to ourselves."

"The room?"

"No," said Jefferson, looking up. He then saw that she was teasing. She knew as well as he did that a relationship between a commanding officer and one of his subordinates was a dangerous thing. Relationships between the officers were tolerated but those between the commander and another were discouraged. Too many problems could arise.

She reached around, behind her neck, and unhooked the top of her dress. She shrugged and it fell over her shoulders. She grabbed it, holding it in place, watching him and smiling at him.

Just then there was a tapping at the door. Jefferson glanced at Norris, but she shook her head telling him that she had ordered nothing. "Who's there?"

"You Colonel Jefferson?"

"Yeah."

"You're ordered to return to the shuttle port. Runner just brought the word."

"You're sure?"

"Look, Colonel, I'm not in the habit of climbing the stairs for no reason and I don't like shouting through doors."

"Thank you," said Jefferson. He then looked at Norris.

"How much time do we have?"

Jefferson looked at his wristwatch but he still hadn't changed it. He glanced at the window but there was no clue about the time there, just the yellow smog-choked glow of the inner city. "I don't know. An hour, maybe."

"Then that's enough time."

"Enough time for what?"

Norris grinned at him evilly and let the front of her dress fall away. She didn't answer.

3

TORRENCE SPOTTED JEFFERSON and Norris standing in one corner of the shuttle terminal watching the crowd. She pointed at them and then waved Sinclair, Lynn, and Carter forward. As she approached, she asked, "What in the hell is going on?"

Jefferson stood silently for a moment, letting Torrence realize that he didn't appreciate being quizzed in that fashion, and then shrugged. "I was told that we had a recall. Immediate. That's all I know."

"Norris?" asked Torrence.

"Why would she know any more than I do?" asked Jefferson.

"Hell, sir, maybe someone told her something important."

A man in the dark blue uniform of the Unified Space Command came toward them. He wore a side arm and a serious look on his deeply tanned face. "Any of you Jefferson?"

"I am."

"Sir, if you'll follow me."

"What about the others?"

"If they'll wait here, we'll get transport arranged. You'll only be gone a few minutes."

"Major Torrence," said Jefferson.

"I'll keep them rounded up. If anyone else shows, I'll keep them right here."

"Lead on then," Jefferson told the man.

They crossed the crowded floor, entered a narrow corridor, and came to the end of it. The man knocked on a door and then opened it without waiting to be invited. "Colonel," he said, waving Jefferson through.

Inside was a single desk, a visitor's chair, and a view screen hung on the wall. Jefferson sat down and waited. A moment later a face appeared.

"Colonel Jefferson?"

"Yes."

"Could you identify yourself, please?"

Jefferson stood and moved closer to the screen. Using his wrist ID, he pressed a slot on the bottom of the screen. A beam scanned his face slowly and then disappeared. A mechanical voice with a slight feminine tinge said, "Jefferson, David Steven, Colonel. ID confirmed."

"Please sit, Colonel."

"Just what in the hell is going on here? We just came off one assignment and were promised a leave on Earth."

"You having a good time on your leave?"

Jefferson shrugged. "So far I haven't had much of a chance to have fun." He thought of the overpriced cab ride and the crowds of people who filled every available square inch of space. He thought of the pollution, the high cost of hotel rooms, and the taste of nearly solid air.

"We have a situation developing and yours is the only unit available."

"On come on," said Jefferson. "I find that hard to believe."

"The problem is that we are restructuring the commands and those units already created and organized are dedicated to other functions. We are caught shorthanded."

Jefferson nodded, understanding exactly what the crap meant. Some paper shuffler, rather than working a little overtime, working a little harder, had noticed that Jefferson and his regiment were available for immediate assignment. It was easier to recall them than to create a new regiment to handle the problem.

"You, with the officers that have been located to this point,

are to report to Shuttle Bay Twelve for transport to the Fifth
Replacement Depot on Station Six at the earliest possible
moment. Your contact, Major Devens, will meet you there and
arrange everything that you need. Questions?"

"What in the hell is going on?"

"That will be answered in the deployment briefing. Anything else?"

Jefferson thought about it. There were a dozen questions he
wanted to ask and knew that each one would be handled with
the same answer. Everything would be available in the deployment briefing. He stood up and shook his head.

"Captain Pulsea will escort you and your officers to the
shuttle. Thank you."

Before Jefferson could say a word, the screen went blank.
He stood looking at it for a moment, waiting for the man to
reappear and tell him a little more. When that didn't happen,
Jefferson turned and left the office.

"Please follow me, Colonel," said Pulsea.

They returned to the others. Rider had returned to the shuttle
port. Rider, the youngest of the company commanders, was
with a woman who looked as if she was barely out of her teens.
She wore shabby clothes, had bare, dirty feet, and looked as if
she hadn't had a good meal in a month or more. She clung to
Rider as if he were a long-lost love she was determined not to
lose again.

"We're ordered back into space," said Jefferson.

"Shit," said Torrence.

"No!" wailed the young woman. "You promised."

"We have very little time," said Pulsea.

Jefferson shot a glance at the man but then nodded. "Let's
get going."

They all picked up their luggage, the little they had.
Spaceflight reduced the number of civilian clothes that each
carried. They figured on buying anything they needed as they
got the chance.

"You promised," yelled the girl. "You promised."

Jefferson turned and saw the woman hanging on to Rider,
trying to hold him back. "Captain," said Jefferson, "I would
suggest that you take care of your problem quietly."

"Problem?" she yelled. "I'm a problem?"

Rider tried to pull free. He kept his voice quiet as he said, "He means your shouting. There is no reason to shout. I've got to make a quick trip up to the station and that's all. It's nothing to get upset about." He turned and appealed to Jefferson. "It will be short, won't it?"

"I believe that we can count on being on the station for no more than a few hours."

"See," said Rider. "Just a few hours."

Now the woman was crying, leaning against Rider's shoulder. He glanced at Jefferson and rolled his eyes. Gently, he pushed the woman away and said, "You wait here for a little while and I'll be back."

"Promise?"

"Of course."

"Captain Rider, if you're finished," said Jefferson. "We do have work to do."

"Yes, sir."

Pulsea moved back through the crowd, taking them toward the shuttle bay. Jefferson was right behind him and the rest of the officers were trailing along, stringing out. As they approached the lock for the bay, Jefferson asked, "What about the enlisted ranks?"

"Recall orders have gone out. Each man or woman has forty-eight hours to reply."

"And if they don't?"

"Then they're left behind."

"Great," said Jefferson. "Nothing like tearing up the Table of Organization and Equipment because of a foul-up in communications. I don't suppose that any provisions have been made to replace critical personnel in the event they don't make the recall."

"You'll have the personnel on the station to draw from."

They stopped at the lock. Jefferson turned and watched as his officers straggled up. Somehow they gained another. Peyton, who hadn't been with the main group, must have seen them heading across the floor and fell in with them.

The lock slid open and the people entered it, waited as it cycled itself, and then the next door opened. They walked out onto the bay floor where the shuttle waited. It looked like an overgrown delta-winged fighter that was capable of flight through the air or into space. Conventional engines lifted it from the ground, taking it higher, into the upper atmosphere where the rockets would take over boosting it into orbit.

Pulsea stopped next to the door and pointed at the open hatch on the shuttle. "They'll take off as soon as you're boarded."

"I'm missing some of my officers."

"They'll be sent as soon as they get here."

Jefferson stood there for a moment, staring at Pulsea, but there was nothing to be read in the man's face. He was a minor official, sent out to do a specific job. He didn't know anything and probably didn't care to know anything.

Without another word to him, Jefferson crossed the grease-and oil-stained floor. At the hatch he was met by a man with a computer-printed list. "You are?"

"Jefferson."

"Yes, sir. I have you manifested through. Please board now for lift-off in just a few minutes."

Jefferson moved to the front, between the two rows of well-worn seats. He sat down, faced the bulkhead in front of him, and saw a splatter about a foot off the floor that might have been almost anything.

Torrence took the seat opposite him and leaned over, into the aisle. "Just what the hell is going on?"

"I don't know," said Jefferson. "Only thing that I've been told is that we're the only unit available for the assignment."

"Sure."

"That's what I said."

As soon as the last of them was on board, the hatch was closed and the steward moved through making sure that everyone had buckled his or her seat belt. Satisfied that the safety regulations were being followed, the steward disappeared into the back. There was no announcement that anything was about to happen. The shuttle shook once and there was a quiet, muted roar in the rear and they began to move slowly.

Jefferson turned and looked out the miniature window. There wasn't much to see. Just a blur of lights and a flash of movement as a truck drove by. He leaned back in the soft, heavily padded chair and waited, feeling cramped. It didn't seem as if there was enough legroom. The curve of the fuselage seemed to come down on the top of his head and the foam of the seat made it next to impossible to shift around for comfort. He glanced at Torrence who seemed to be perfectly relaxed and envied her the ability. He hated the shuttle, knowing that a mistake could splatter them over a couple of square miles of open land.

They left the confines of the terminal and burst out into the open air, taxiing along. Now everything had a yellow cast to it. Sunlight through the layers of smog. Jefferson turned and focused his attention on the bulkhead, not wanting to know what was happening outside the shuttle.

They reached the end of the runway, positioned themselves on it, and then sat for a moment. Slowly, the noise of the engines increased until the whole of the shuttle was vibrating with power. Jefferson was forced back into the seat as the shuttle surged forward and began to race down the runway. Cool air, forced through the nozzles above his head, added to the sensation of motion. There was a buffeting as the wheels tried to break free from the rough concrete and then, suddenly, they were airborne, the forces on his body changing as they climbed steeply, first toward the sun, and then to one side of it.

Jefferson's stomach seemed to vibrate with the shuttle. He felt a cold sweat blossom on his head. He clamped his teeth together, certain that he was going to throw up, but then they were into the smooth air and the rumbling of the jets was left behind them. He turned toward the window. Bright sunlight was streaming in now. Not the dirty yellow of the smog-filtered sun, but the clean, bright light from above the smog layer. It was a smudge below the shuttle that obscured the ground.

"Well, we're off again," said Torrence.

Jefferson glanced at her. As usual, she seemed cool and calm. Nothing ever got to her. Battle situations thrown at her were shrugged off as she responded to them. She ignored discomfort and danger and even the terror of enemy forces attacking. She just kept firing until her adversary was down and the attack was broken. Nothing bothered her.

"I hate this," said Jefferson.

"I can see that."

"No," he said. "You don't understand. Here, I'm at the mercy of the pilots. Did they cheat their way through school?

Did one of them have a fight with the wife or the husband and now is so mad that he or she can't think straight? Maybe one has a death wish? Maybe the maintenance crew wasn't as well trained as they might have been. All things that I can't control. I have to rely on so many people that I don't know to do their jobs right, not to mention that most of the shuttles were built by the lowest bidders."

"With that attitude," said Torrence, "I'm surprised that you even get on one of these."

Jefferson grinned weakly. "I wanted to see Earth again."

Torrence glanced at the window and then back at him. "Was it worth it?"

"Nope. They haven't learned a damned thing. You'd think they'd see the solutions. Obvious solutions. But they're doing nothing to change things except ship people off planet."

"That is one way to handle it," she said.

"Not the best."

"No, I suppose not."

There was a bong and a voice came on the intercom. "We are entering the upper reaches of the atmosphere. We are, basically, in space."

"That's what I wanted to hear," said Jefferson.

"We will be docking at Station Six in just over an hour. Please remain seated and keep your safety harness fastened."

The shuttle pilot was as good as his word. Within an hour they were on short approach toward Station Six. They landed in the shuttle bay and were met by the shuttle-way, a sealed tube that allowed them to walk from the wide-open shuttle bay into the station proper. Once they were there, another officer met them, telling Jefferson and Torrence, along with Carter, the intelligence officer, that they had a briefing immediately. The rest of the staff would be shown to a temporary regimental area where they could begin organizing the regimental personnel.

They weren't given much of a chance to look around, but Jefferson did notice the difference between the station and everything on the ground. There were no people sleeping in the corridors. The floors were clean and the walls had been painted recently. There were some tubes, conduits for wires or various gases needed to operate the station. But the point was, the air was breathable, even if it did have a slightly metallic tang, the temperature was comfortable, and there wasn't the stench of humanity pressed into areas that were too small for the number of people present.

Their escort opened a hatch and gestured toward the interior. "The general will be in to see you in a few minutes."

Jefferson entered expecting to find a conference room—a table surrounded by chairs, a holotank, and a map or two. Instead there were large chairs that looked as if they would swallow anyone who sat in them. The lighting was muted so that it was dark in the room.

"Be seated," said the escort.

Jefferson sat down. His view was limited by the wings of the chair. He could see toward the holotank. A moment later a burst of color sprang from the tank, hovered in the air like a cloud, and then slowly coalesced into the shape of the general. It looked directly at Jefferson.

"I'm sorry that you had to cut your leave short, Colonel, but we have a situation developing."

"Yes, General," said Jefferson. "I've been told that but nothing more than that."

"We'll get into that in a moment. First, let me welcome you back to duty and to Station Six. And let me assure you that provisions are being made for your return to leave just as soon as the current crisis is resolved."

"Thank you, General." Jefferson wanted to glance at the others, but couldn't see them because of the chairs. He knew that he was sounding like the biggest suck-ass in military history, but there really was nothing else for him to do. Complaining to the general would only get him into trouble and nothing would be accomplished. They had to hear the assignment and then later, if there was a chance, mention to the inspector general that the treatment hadn't been fair.

"I know that you're all busy," said the general's shape, "so I won't keep you. Questions will be answered at the end of the session."

There was a pop and the general was gone. Jefferson was sure the pop was some kind of special effects nonsense to get their attention and to make the general's departure that much more dramatic.

The shimmering cloud of color over the holotank solidified, changed, and then became the outline of a solar system. A voice that came from nowhere said, "This is the Zeti Alpha-seven System approximately three hundred and thirty-seven light-years from Earth. It is part of a double star system with the partner no more than three quarters of a light-year away. It is, however, a dim partner, not much brighter than Venus at its brightest."

"Great," said a voice from behind Jefferson.

"There are thirteen planets in the system, dozens of moons, and a single asteroid belt that is probably more of an Oort Cloud than an asteroid belt."

"Same difference," mumbled Torrence.

"There are two planets inside the star's biosphere. The first is inhabited by local intelligent creatures that have developed a rudimentary spaceflight . . . interplanetary flight, and they have attempted to colonize the second."

There was a moment's hesitation and the voice said, "What I mean is that the second planet in order from the star is the first in the biosphere and the third is the second. I mean intelligence developed on the second and spread to the third."

"Thanks for clearing that up," said Jefferson sarcastically.

"Since there was no indigenous intelligence on the third planet and since its climate, size, and atmosphere approximated Earth's, it was targeted for colonization by our government. Colonists were recruited and dispatched."

"Oh, shit," said Jefferson. "Some asshole got himself into trouble."

Again there was a hesitation and the voice said, "Please, sir, don't interrupt. I lose my place."

"Just skip on down," said Jefferson. "What's the bottom line here."

"Our colonists maintain a radio link with home and there are various emergency signals that can be broadcast if there is trouble."

"Which would take over three hundred years for us to receive," said Jefferson.

"If the signal was heard on Earth. A picket ship picked it up and a courier brought it in. According to that, one of the bases was under attack and help was requested."

"Flyby?" said Jefferson, knowing that SOP would detail the picket ship to ascertain if the signal was legitimate or if it had been sent by accident.

"Accomplished. The colony had been attacked. Bodies were spotted on sensors. All electronics were down. Computers failed to respond. Since the picket did not contain sufficient personnel to land and recon, the request for an operational regiment to return and survey the situation from the ground was made by the picket."

"Shit," said Jefferson. "Unknown trouble call."

"Yes, sir," said the voice. "I'm afraid that's exactly what we've got."

4

LUCAS REARDON CROUCHED in the thorn-studded thicket, trying to hide himself in the shadows while the natives beat the bush looking for him. Tall, slender natives with bullet-shaped heads, long arms that hung nearly to their knees, and hands with fingers that were long and loose and might be called tentacles. Foul, evil creatures who didn't respect human life or any life for that matter. At least that was what Reardon now believed.

Reardon slowly raised a hand and wiped the sweat from his face. He rubbed it on his torn shirt and tried to make no noise. He didn't know if the creatures could hear him. He didn't know if they could smell him. During the six months he'd been there, he'd had little contact with them. They were ugly, stupid, and didn't deserve the time they tried to demand. Now they were hunting him in a fairly systematic way.

He shifted around and saw two of them freeze, looking toward him. Not wanting to give his position away, he stopped moving and tried to stop breathing. He wanted to drop flat and bury himself in the soft soil of the planet but didn't want to move again. He didn't want to do a thing that would draw attention to himself.

The two aliens stood still, their heads swiveling as if they were mounted on poles. They spoke to each other, the language sounding like the mewing of kittens. Then one of them pointed, his arm out straight, and a rising moan came from him almost like a siren just beginning to sound.

Reardon wanted to sink to the ground but was afraid to move. Afraid that the aliens could see well in the dark and any movement would draw their attention to him. Then, off to the right, a hundred yards away, there was a sudden commotion, the rattling of branches as something rose up and began to run. A human, fleeing from the creatures.

The two closest to him raised rifles. Laser rifles that he believed stolen when they had overrun the camp. The ruby-colored beams flashed, burning through the night. The branch of a tree was severed and crashed. Another absorbed the beam and then burst into flame. But the fleeing figure continued to run, dodging right and left as it worked its way up a hill and then disappeared on the other side.

As it vanished, the two creatures stopped shooting. They glanced at each other and then began to run forward, loping up the hill in a running, jumping stride that seemed to eat the distance.

When the creatures were gone, Reardon struggled out of the thicket. The thorns ripped at his clothes and his skin. The scratches burned, as if a mild acid were poured into the wound. Ignoring the pain, he crawled free and stood up.

With the aliens running after that other person, whoever it might have been, Reardon knew what he had to do. He turned and began walking in the opposite direction. He stayed in the shadows, falling to the ground frequently, listening for signs that the creatures were coming back at him. Listening for evidence that he was being followed or was about to be captured, but there was nothing except the quiet breeze rattling through the trees overhead and the distant screams as the creatures shouted at each other.

Jefferson sat in the tiny regimental office, a computer screen to his right, the screen glowing green. It was a continuously updated list of the personnel who had reported in and were now on their way back to the shuttle port or who were already on their way to the Replacement Depot.

Glancing at the clock on the bulkhead above the hatch, Torrence said. "We've got just under forty-one hours left."

Without a word to her, Jefferson leaned forward and tapped the keyboard, waited as the screen cleared and new information was displayed. "We're now at forty-two percent of our strength. We're critical in weapons and in two infantry companies."

"Infantry's easy to replace," said Torrence. "Warm bodies holding a rifle. The weapons specialists might give us some headaches."

Suddenly Jefferson felt tired. One minute he'd been downtown on Earth about to have some real fun and the next he was on a shuttle heading back to work. No decompression. Just a sudden shift in priorities. Now everything was on a rush basis. Do this now. Organize the regiment now. Get the people back and ready to move in now. He rubbed his eyes and felt a burning behind his eyelids.

"We're not going to make it," he said.

Torrence ignored that. "Officer strength is nearly full. Of the primary staff, only Winston has failed to respond. Oh, and we still don't have a permanent replacement for Mitchell."

"What about his exec?"

"Woman was wounded badly and I don't think she's available either."

"I'll pass on that now."

Torrence glanced at the lap-top. "Then the only real problem now is that video guy, Garvey. He's back."

"Great. That's all we need."

Torrence shrugged. "A little good press for us and we could wind up as generals."

"And a story slanted slightly wrong and we could wind up in jail."

"He's here, has quarters, and has been authorized to accompany us."

"Then I'll stay quiet," said Jefferson.

Torrence closed the lap-top and said, "That's it then."

"You have a chance to examine the personnel available in case we're missing some critical specialty?"

"The people here all have job skills that relate to the operation of the station. If our weapons people fail to show, there isn't much here to use for replacement." She waved a hand. "Oh, there is some gross crossover but nothing that's going to be real beneficial."

"Fine. You can go."

"Where will you be?"

Jefferson shrugged and pointed at the computer screen. "Right here watching the progress of the various departments and personnel."

The buzzing of the desk phone brought him awake. He reached out, touched the activate button, and waited. A face appeared and announced, "Deployment briefing in five minutes. Hurry." Before Jefferson could respond, the screen went dark.

He glanced at the computer screen and learned that fifty-seven percent of his regiment had been located and were either on the station or en route to it. Just fifty-seven percent. He knew what was happening. Men and women on leave just didn't respond to sudden recalls quickly. If they ignored the summons and could show that it had never reached them, then they were free and clear. Their leaves would remain intact and they would be assigned to other units on their return to duty.

He knew that it meant that better than forty percent of the people assigned to him had no real esprit. They didn't care about the unit or their friends in it. They wanted to stay on Earth for their leaves.

And that was something that Jefferson couldn't understand. Earth was a pit. A hot, pollution-choked pit where everything was overpriced and overrated. Accommodations on the ships were luxurious compared to everything on Earth. It made no sense that people would want to stay there. Yet forty percent of his regiment seemed to have taken that course.

He reached over and snapped off the computer. He dimmed the lights in the office and stepped into the corridor. The normally white lights were now glowing red. It was nighttime. The station was set to a standard twenty-four-hour day so that the biological rhythms of the soldiers wouldn't be too badly thrown off.

He walked down the corridor, again amazed at the cleanliness. No strong odors that threatened to sicken. No people trying to find a little clear space in which to stretch out.

Recycled air that somehow smelled artificial but infinitely better than the pollution-ladened atmosphere on Earth.

He entered the briefing room and found Torrence already there, holding a cup of coffee in both hands as if she was trying to warm them with the cup. Sinclair, Carter, and Peyton were also present.

"What's happening?" he asked.

Torrence shrugged and as she did a voice from the holotank said, "Be seated. Let's get started."

Jefferson looked longingly at the cup of coffee that Torrence held, but there was no sign of coffee in the conference room. It was something that she had brought with her.

Jefferson moved forward and took his seat. The holotank shimmered and flashed and the star system they had been shown only hours before came back into focus. A red arrow, looking like a moon, hung in the simulated sky, pointing at the third planet in the system.

"The situation has deteriorated in the last few hours," said the voice. "Deployment of the regiment is now planned for no later than oh-nine-three-oh this morning."

"Christ, that's less than six hours," said Carter.

Jefferson stood up. "Carter, this is your field of expertise. I want you to remain here for a full briefing and then be prepared to inform Major Torrence and me as soon as possible."

From the holotank the voice said, "Colonel Jefferson, I would suggest that you remain for this complete briefing."

"No," said Jefferson. "There is too much work to be done and too little time to do it."

"Colonel," said the voice.

Jefferson ignored it. "I want the entire regiment assembled by oh-seven-hundred and I want a face-to-face count cross-checked against the computer. Torrence, you and Winston get together and start screening people to fill in the critical specialties."

"Winston still isn't here."

"Then get with his deputy, but I want those critical shortages filled."

"Yes, sir."

He hesitated, looking back at the holotank. The red arrow was shimmering above the planet's surface that was glowing a pale yellowish green. He knew that he would pay for not listening to the briefing, but then there would be time on the ship during the trip for that. Now there were more important things to be done.

"Let's get at it," he said.

The next few hours were frantic. People were running around. Calls were flashing in and the computer continued to demand attention with a hundred details. Winston wasn't found. Peyton and Norris ran around the station, Peyton checking operational details and Norris making sure that all equipment required and assigned was being loaded.

Jefferson tried to count the boxes being loaded into the cargo ship but couldn't get close enough. Norris was standing there, a computer list in one hand as she checked through the crates. When he failed to learn anything important, he retreated to his office and punched up the computerized personnel list. More of the regiment had been located but two of the shuttles would not dock before the fleet lifted into deep space.

Jefferson punched up the general staff and got the operations officer, Colonel Nichols. Jefferson told him, "I'd like to delay my departure by two hours."

"Negative," said Nichols.

"Just like that? No questions about it. Just negative."

"Departure is scheduled when departure is scheduled."

"I'll be missing part of the regiment."

"Military units have been fielded in the past at less than full strength."

"Granted, but given that we've a long trip ahead of us I don't understand this sudden need for speed."

"The general desires it."

Jefferson nodded and understood that. The general had decided that the regiment would be deployed at a specific time and that was the way it had to be. Unless there was a good reason to delay departure.

"We won't be ready on time."

"I would suggest, Colonel, that you be ready on time," said Nichols.

"I have people en route who won't make the departure."

"Sounds like a personal problem."

"Colonel Nichols, I fail to see how a delay of two hours is going to foul up any scheduling. The delay will allow some critical people to arrive."

"Departure time stands. Period. You have any other questions?"

Jefferson stared at the hard face on the screen, searching for some humanity in it, and realized that there was none. For the first time in weeks he thought of Sergeant Mason, killed when he, Jefferson, had won his medal. The one that got him everything he now had. Sergeant Mason would tell him that there was no sense in battering his face against a brick wall when there was absolutely no chance of breaking the wall. Let it go and do the best you could with what you had.

"No, Colonel. We'll depart on time."

"The general will be pleased."

Jefferson hit the disconnect button and looked up to see Torrence standing there. "Well?" he said.

"Equipment is loaded and ready. Muster is completed. We're now at fifty-nine percent strength. About fifty-fifty on the critical stuff."

Jefferson looked at the clock above the bulkhead, surprised that the time had slipped away so quickly. "Everyone on board the ships?"

"Everyone except those who have functions that require them here."

"Let's pass the word to get everyone ready to go."

"Yes, sir." She turned and got out.

Jefferson stood up and then faced the computer. It was continuing to monitor the progress, showing more of the task completed even with the gaps in personnel. He reached over and shut it off. He glanced around one last time, like a man in a hotel making sure that he had left nothing of himself in the impersonal room.

He left the office, walked the corridor, and wondered about the quarters that had been assigned to him but that he'd never seen. He stayed close to the wall, using it to protect his right side as if fearing attack from there. The red lights were gone, replaced by white. Day had return to the station.

As he approached the loading dock on the outside of the station, he saw that his officers were clustered there waiting.

As he approached them, two of them ducked down to crawl through the hatch. Torrence waited.

"Regiment, such as it is, is formed and ready for transport," she said formally.

"Then let's get this show on the road."

"Yes, sir."

Torrence crawled into the hatch. Jefferson stood there for a moment, thinking that there must be some historic words that should be spoken. This was a historic moment. A regiment about to be sent into space to fight some as yet unidentified menace. Words were necessary. But Jefferson had none and there was now no one around to hear them. As soon as Torrence and the others were out of the way, Jefferson crouched and crawled into the tunnel thinking that it was an undignified way to enter a ship and to fly off into history. But then again, there was no one to see that either.

When he entered the other ship there was an officer who said, "This way, Colonel."

And once again, Jefferson was being led off to his destiny. He wondered why he suddenly felt like a calf being led to slaughter. He followed along and hoped that his premonition would not come true.

5

THE ALIEN STOOD with its back to him, watching something in the far distance. It held a laser rifle in its left hand. The clothing was leather, a strange green that looked as if it had once belonged to a lizard. Around its thick waist was a belt holding a small pack that might contain food and something that could be a canteen. Any of the items would be valuable to his survival. Reardon didn't know how much longer he could survive without some kind of help.

Reardon was measuring the distances and the angles, wondering if he could get to the creature and kill it before it sensed his approach and used the laser on him. He shifted to the right and flattened himself on the ground. The moisture soaked through the rags that were his clothes. He was suddenly aware of the sounds around him. Quiet buzzings like that of bees on Earth. A sharp call that might have been a bird or a lizard or something that he had never seen before.

He shook his head, trying to drive the noises from it. The creature was all that he wanted to see. His whole attention was focused on it. A single being standing there as if on guard, not moving.

As he started to come up, onto the balls of his feet and his hands, ready to make the last dashing run, he wondered if it was a trap. The alien knew he was out there and wanted him to attack. Wanted him to try to get to it so that it could burn him down. The distance was fifteen, twenty feet, but that was plenty of space for the alien to operate.

Then, in the distance, at the very edge of a finger of forest that reached up and over the top of a hill, Reardon caught a flash of movement. That was what held the creature's attention. Something moving in the distance.

With that Reardon was up on his feet, running forward. He no longer cared about making noise or warning the alien. His goal was in front of him. Four feet away, he leapt, screaming. That was enough of a warning for the creature. It ducked instinctively and tried to whirl. Reardon crashed into it, but his feet missed the vital parts. A foot glanced from its shoulder. Both of them went down, the alien losing its grip on the laser rifle.

Reardon rolled free and leapt to his feet. He faced the alien, crouched, his hands out, fingers spread like a wrestler waiting for the beginning of the match. He watched as the alien struggled to stand. It turned to face him and as it did, Reardon attacked again. He kicked at the crotch, but his foot struck solid bone. Pain flared in his foot and up his leg. He fell and rolled away.

The alien came at him but didn't seem to understand the finer points of hand-to-hand fighting. It reached out slowly and Reardon ducked under the hand. He scrambled right and then kicked again, this time trying to sweep the creature's feet out from under it.

As it fell, Reardon pounced, landing on the creature's chest. It grunted in surprise and then tried to roll over. When that failed, it just sat up, throwing Reardon away, demonstrating incredible upper body strength. As Reardon tumbled off the creature, his right hand struck the barrel of the laser rifle. Reardon grabbed it, rolled over, and leapt to his feet. He ran ten or twelve yards and then whirled. The alien was sitting on the ground, both hands held to its head. Reardon aimed and fired. The beam flashed brightly and briefly and the alien fell back, dead.

Reardon dropped to one knee then, his head down. The breath was ragged in his throat. Sweat had blossomed and soaked his clothes. He closed his eyes momentarily and tried to clear his mind. Then opened them and moved to the body. Searching the belt pockets, he found little that was of use to him. Things that he didn't understand. Small metallic devices that might have been coins or might have been something else entirely. He found no food or water, but then he did have the laser rifle.

He turned then, looking back toward the finger of forest, but whatever had drawn the attention of the alien was gone. Still, the forest was a better place to be than the somewhat open ground where he stood now. Although the light had faded, he would still be a target. He had to get out of the open. He turned and started walking toward the forest, moving slowly.

As the last of the light faded, he reached the forest. It seemed cooler there. The odors were different too. Musty, like the basement of an old house that had leaked rain all summer. The trees were alive with creatures running among the branches, leaping from one tree to another, scolding one another. They rattled the leaves, drawing his attention up to them, but he couldn't see them now. It was too dark.

Reardon sat down on the damp soil, his back to one of the trees. The laser rifle was across his knees. Hunger gnawed at his belly, but it was no longer the blinding, nerve-deadening pain it had been. He was beyond that stage. Now it was a numbness. A numbness that was always there. It was that he was afraid to eat anything. Their survival classes had always been predicated on a quick rescue. Either someone from the fleet found them or they reached another Earth outpost. No one had talked about survival in the alien jungle without food.

The theory just hadn't worked. The radio signal had been sent but no fleet had arrived. No one had arrived. Reardon closed his eyes and let his mind roam. For days, weeks, hell, it could have been months for all he knew, he had avoided thinking about it. Thinking about the destruction of the camp and the deaths of his fellows, but now it all crowded in on him, replaying in his mind like a movie seen night after night on the video.

He still didn't understand how they had short-circuited the defensive system. Mere tampering with it was supposed to trigger it. But that hadn't happened. It had been shut down so that they wouldn't be killing the migrating animals, but then he'd recognized the danger. The system had been activated and still the enemy had managed to get inside the stockade, and once they were in, the slaughter started.

Reardon had stayed in the control booth watching. Alien creatures with old-fashioned slug-throwing rifles, firing at anything and everything. The men had come boiling out of their quarters, armed with lasers, but those had done no good. At close quarters, the old rifles were as good as the lasers. Automatic weapons equalized the advantage that lasers were supposed to provide so that sheer numbers of people or aliens became important and Reardon's people were outnumbered. Badly.

The fight had gone well at first. They'd held their own, and if the defensive system had kicked in at any moment, they might have won. But too many aliens got inside and then the humans began dying a little too quickly. One man had gone down under a hail of bullets that ripped him apart. Another was overwhelmed by aliens. They had beat him to the ground, stomping him until he was dead.

The aliens started breaking into the rooms, into the houses of the people. A few aliens died right there, pierced by laser fire. Other creatures were clubbed down, falling into broken, bleeding heaps, but there were always others to follow the first. They would swarm the houses, crashing through the windows or smashing down the doors to finally emerge triumphant, holding the booty high as if it was some kind of award for being brave and daring.

Reardon had crouched in the door of the guard shack using his laser rifle. He had to be careful with it. One shot could easily pierce an alien and then hit a human. Short, quick shots directed at the creatures when they were in the clear.

But even as he fired, he knew that it was hopeless. Too many of the aliens were in the camp. Even with the automatic emergency signal being broadcast, it was too late. It was hopeless. So, rather than stay there to be killed with his fellows, Reardon had decided to get out.

To flee.

To run.

He'd turned and saw that Garnett was gone, probably out to

help his family. Reardon had hit a button that opened the doors scattered around the stockade. He didn't think that he was suddenly allowing the aliens access to the camp. Hell, they were already inside. What he was doing was providing those with enough sense to get out the means to do just that.

Outside the battle was beginning to wane. Firing from the lasers had slowed. The detonations of the weapons carried by the aliens filled the night. Muzzle flashes strobed lighting corners of the compound like the winking of a giant camera. These scenes were frozen in time in Reardon's mind. Dead men and women on the ground. Blood-soaked bodies ignored by everyone.

Reardon then slipped from the guard shack and worked his way along the stockade, sticking to the shadows. He froze once as an alien ran past him, a low growl coming from its throat. As it vanished around a corner, Reardon moved, and then ran for an open door. He dived through it, rolled to the right, and lay still.

For an instant it seemed that he had gotten out cleanly, but then a single shot snapped by his head. Not knowing where it had come from, Reardon scrambled up and ran. He tossed his rifle away, not wanting it to slow him down. He ran straight away from the camp, heading toward the distant trees. He ran with his head down and his arms pumping. He ran as hard as he could and as fast as he could, ignoring the noise coming from the stockade, ignoring the firing of the weapons and the screaming of the people. He ran until he was sure that he would reach the woods and then he slowed slightly, trying to catch his breath.

Once in the safety of the forest, he stopped. He crouched and then leaned forward, his arm against the smooth trunk of a tree, his forehead on his arm. Pain from the sprint radiated from his chest up into this arms. It felt like a massive heart attack, but then his breathing slowed and the pain faded and all that remained was the sweat soaking his body.

Slowly, he got to his feet and looked back. There were fires burning in the stockade now and the automatic fire-fighting equipment was not responding. Flames were shooting fifty, a hundred feet into the air. There were alarms sounding, but no evidence that anyone was left to fight the fires.

Reardon waited for a few minutes, hoping that others had gotten out, but no one appeared on the open ground. Finally, believing that he was the only survivor, he turned and walked deeper into the forest, hoping that putting distance between the stockade and himself would allow him to live a little longer. Just a little longer.

Now Reardon opened his eyes and stared into the new forest. There was a new pain in his belly, but this one wasn't from hunger or fear. It was disgust. Disgust with himself for being the coward that he was. Disgust that he had run rather than staying to fight. Disgust that he had opened the doors that allowed more of the enemy in. Disgust that he had not died nobly with his fellows.

Shaking himself, he stood up, telling himself that he was smart and he was lucky. There was only one thing that he needed now. Water. That was all he needed. He tried to focus his attention on that because he suddenly didn't like the direction his mind was taking him.

But even as he was up and moving, walking, feeling his way through the darkened forest, another thought came to him unbidden. That was the second camp. The second stockade.

The humans had spread them out, across the main land mass from the shallow bay that was perfect for a shuttle landing site, eastward, and up, into the mountains. A dozen such camps, each with its own stockade and defense and everything else it needed, spread over the land so that the humans had a line of communication from the mountains to the sea.

So Reardon, knowing that, had run, walked, crawled, toward the next camp in the chain, knowing that help would be there. All he had to do was reach it and there would be hot food, cold drink, and protection. Safety was something less than a hundred miles from his ruined home. An hour on a speeder but now days away.

But when he'd reached it, there had been no hot food or cold drink or safety. There had been a smoking ruin with the bodies of the human inhabitants scattered on the ground. The buildings had been ransacked, the contents strewn everywhere. Anything the aliens could use had been carried off. Everything else had been destroyed.

Reardon sat down in the middle of the destruction and felt

like crying. Slowly he turned his head. The body of a child lay crumpled near the wall of a house. Two men lying near a door, one of them missing his head. A computer, the screen shattered and the shards of glass spread around it like pools of blood around the dead.

And then Reardon realized that he was crying, the tears streaming down his cheeks. He was overwhelmed by the sadness. Promises of a better life off Earth had been made. A chance to live a life without the poverty, the pollution, the danger that held Earth in its grip. A chance to make something. To build something. And now that was all gone as alien beings ran loose killing and looting.

As the night came, Reardon had gotten to his feet. He had searched a couple of the houses looking for anything of value that the aliens might have overlooked. He found some freeze dried food still sealed in its packets. He drank some water from the well and he found a single knife. The blade was broken but there was enough of it left that it might be useful.

With his treasures, he had gotten out of the camp, afraid that the aliens might come back. He had walked through the night, holing up at the first sign of the morning sun. He ate some of the food, drank more of the water, and then had gone to sleep, his mind blank.

From that moment on, he had been unsure what to do. It seemed that each of the camps would have been attacked and only the one at the shuttle landing site, near the shallow bay, would have the strength to survive. Only that one. And it was more than a thousand miles away. It would take weeks of walking to reach the bay, if he could find it. If he was lucky.

Again, Reardon didn't like the direction his mind was taking him. Water was what he needed. That was all that he needed at the moment. He didn't need to think about opening doorways to escape or fleeing into the night like a coward. All he had to concentrate on was finding water and then living for just another day because if he could do that, then he might be rescued. Help had to be coming.

As he dropped to his knees near a shallow stream of slowly moving water, he thought about rescue again. It had to be coming. It just had to.

6

JEFFERSON SAT IN the quarters assigned to him, impressed with the luxury of them, especially when compared to the four-hundred-dollar room he had seen on Earth. Here there was a bed that folded up into the bulkhead so that it was out of the way during the day. There was an easy chair bolted to the metal floor and a desk that held a computer. A chair on a swivel and slotted into the floor sat near it. There was a slight alcove that contained the toilet facility and a stand-up shower that held four gallons of recycled water. As he washed himself, the water drained, was filtered, and pumped right back up through the shower head. A closed system that lost only a small amount of water to evaporation during the shower.

Such luxury when compared to life on Earth. Sure luxury when compared to the enlisted quarters that were little more than coffin-sized boxes where the men and women could get a little privacy for a few hours.

There was a tap on the hatch and Jefferson leaned over to touch the access button that opened the hatch. There were such buttons in easy reach scattered around the cabin. No one wanted the commander to have to move a couple of feet to open up for visitors.

Courtney Norris entered. She stopped, centered herself, and

said in a voice loud enough for anyone in the corridor outside
to hear, "Lieutenant Norris reporting as ordered."

But then the hatch swung shut automatically with a quiet
clang and as it did, Norris reached up for the Velcro fastenings
on her jumpsuit. "You did order me to report, didn't you,
Colonel?"

Jefferson shook his head. "Not that I remember." He
grinned at her. "That was a nice touch though."

"I thought you'd like it." She pulled at the Velcro. The
sound of it coming apart was nearly as loud as the roaring of a
volcanic eruption.

"Jesus," said Jefferson, surprised at his sudden response. He
was like a teenager being seduced for the first time.

"Maybe we have time to finish what we started on Earth,"
said Norris.

Jefferson nodded dumbly, thinking that he should end it right
there, right now. Meeting with a staff officer on Earth was one
thing. That was separated from the command structure if only
because it was on Earth while they were on leave. Now they
were on the ship, in space, and he should end it all.

But Norris had pulled the top of her jumpsuit apart in much
the same fashion that she had used to take off her dress while
on Earth and Jefferson knew that it was too late. She'd gotten
to him before he had a chance to act.

"What are you thinking?" she asked.

Jefferson almost told her and then thought better of it.
Instead he said, "How beautiful you look."

"Why thank you."

And then the screen on the desk beeped, signaling him that
someone wanted to talk to him. Jefferson turned his eyes
toward the screen and said, "Shit."

Norris pulled her jumpsuit up and fastened the Velcro as
Jefferson moved to the desk. He glanced at her making sure
that she was covered and that she couldn't be seen. Then he sat
down and touched the call button. "Jefferson here."

"Captain would like to see you on the bridge."

"Now?"

"Yes, sir. If it is convenient."

"Be about ten minutes," said Jefferson. He touched the
button and the screen darkened.

"Thanks," said Norris.

"Nothing I can do about that."

"I thought you were in command," she said.

"Well, there you get into a tricky situation. I command the unit and have ultimate responsibility for everything, everyone, and all the equipment, but while we're in space the captain of the ship has the final word where it involves the operation of the ship or the safety of it."

"What about a tactical situation," asked Norris.

Jefferson grinned. "Well, technically, I think that I command but then I could always be overruled by the captain telling me that the safety of the ship has come into play, not to mention the fact that I'm not well versed in the tactics of fighting in outer space. As I say, it's a tricky situation."

"So he summons and you run off."

Jefferson turned and faced her. He wiped a hand over his face and said, "The captain would not summon me if it wasn't important. Therefore, I should go."

Norris took a deep breath and sat down in the chair. "Should I wait?"

There was a tap at the hatch. Jefferson glanced at it and then at Norris. "Let's be discreet here. Maybe it would be better if you left. If it doesn't take long, I'll send a corporal down to tell you to report. All businesslike."

The tap came again and Jefferson touched the button. "Yes?"

"Major Torrence here. Captain has requested us on the bridge."

"I'm aware of that, Major. Wait one." Jefferson stood up and then took a computer module from his desk. "Here. Carry that around to make it look official."

She took it but then asked, "You think we're fooling anyone with this sort of thing?"

"I certainly hope so." He moved to the hatch. Norris joined him and he opened it. As he stepped out, he said, "I'll want a full report tonight . . . tomorrow morning at the latest."

"Yes, sir." Norris hurried down the corridor without greeting Torrence.

"What was that all about?"

Jefferson glanced at his second in command and said, "Nothing important."

"We have a problem with the equipment or the replacements?"

"I just wanted Norris to run a quick check to make sure that nothing was damaged in the rush to get everything on the ship. That's all."

Torrence shot him a glance, surprised by the tone of his voice. "That's all?"

"Yes, Major. Now, let's get going."

They walked along the corridors, lighted by dim red bulbs since the ship was in its nighttime mode. They took an elevator up and exited on the bridge. It was the first time that Jefferson had been on the bridge of a warship and he was surprised by it.

There was, of course, a screen situated to the front so that it looked like an old-fashioned theater, but the screen showed space outside the ship. There was nothing interesting to see except the distant stars and one small marble-sized planet floating at the lower edge of it.

Two crew members were sitting at a huge monitoring station. There were half a dozen small screens in front of them and two panels that held various buttons, switches, and knobs. There was another station next to them and a third on the other side of the elevator. A helmsman sat to one side with a navigator near him. And right in the middle of it all, with a chair that swiveled a full three hundred and sixty degrees, was the captain. From his chair, he could see each monitor and control head. He could see everything that he had to and he could run every aspect of the ship from that chair if he had to.

Jefferson moved forward and said, "You wanted to see us, Captain?"

Captain Jack Clemens turned and faced them. He was a thin man with greying hair. Unlike Jefferson who was a contemporary of his troops, Clemens was older by several years. He had brown eyes, a pointed nose, and a high voice.

"Ah, Colonel Jefferson. I hope you don't mind but I took the liberty of alerting your second in command."

"That's fine."

The captain waved them forward and then seemed to lower

his voice. "I'm afraid that the situation has changed significantly in the last twenty-four hours."

Jefferson nodded, thought of a hundred questions, and then didn't ask a one of them.

"We're going to have to punch up the speed and to do that your people are going to have to go into suspension."

"I had counted on having an opportunity for some training on the voyage," said Jefferson.

"We've got to make some time," said the captain. "The situation is getting worse."

"Just what in the hell is going on?" asked Jefferson.

The captain turned and pointed at one of his officers. "Lieutenant Tabor, if you please."

Tabor stood up. She was a short, stocky woman with short brown hair. She moved toward the captain's chair and said, "Yes, sir?"

"What has been going on out in the Zeta Alpha-seven System?"

"Second emergency signal and no response from either of the bases. There are reports of ships in space overhead, visible on the long-range scans," she said. Then she looked up and added, "I don't know the significance of this, but there have been protests from the European community."

"Flybys?" asked Jefferson, feeling that he had been there before.

"Bases have been eliminated through hostile action. That is all we know," said Tabor.

"What's the problem?" asked Torrence.

"Distances. We're talking about light-years."

Jefferson shook his head. "There are fleets available and there have to be scout craft."

"Yes, sir," said Tabor. "Except that no one has been diverted. We're talking about remote probes and information that is radioed back. Everything takes time."

Now the captain interrupted. "It boils down to us being the very scout that you think should have been sent. We're going to find out what happened."

Jefferson shook his head. "I don't like this."

"I understand that," said the captain. He glanced at his officer. "Anything else?"

"Our responsibility is to learn what happened and protect human lives. Especially protect human lives."

"I know that," said Jefferson.

The captain nodded and said, "Because of that, and the escalating nature of the problem, we've been ordered to make as much speed as possible."

Jefferson turned and looked at the screen. The marble-sized planet was still in the corner, but now he could see the light rings around it. He studied the whole screen, the stars just small points of light.

"How long before we arrive on station?"

"If we make as much speed as possible, just over three weeks."

"And we'll be the first ships on station?"

The captain nodded. "There was no one else available."

Jefferson turned and faced him. "Can we expect more information at some point?"

Tabor fielded that one. She grinned and said, "The nice thing about heading in is that we'll run into the signals transmitted from the system. We're hoping that we'll learn something once we intercept those signals."

"If we can get battened down quickly, we can begin the acceleration."

Jefferson glanced at Torrence. "Take us an hour to get everything set."

"Please inform me when you have completed your preparations."

Jefferson nodded and then headed toward the elevator. He hesitated at the doors and when Torrence joined him, he said, "Can we do it in an hour?"

"Shouldn't be a problem, sir. Spread the word down through the chain of command. Doesn't take that long to set it up."

"I don't like losing the training time," said Jefferson.

"Nothing we can do about it," said Torrence.

"Nope," agreed Jefferson. "Nothing at all."

At the end of the hour, Jefferson stood in one of the company bays watching as the last of the officers sealed himself into his cube. He adjusted the two hoses, color coded, that would allow the suspension gases in and the respiratory gases out. Once he was in place, Jefferson would retreat, seal the bay, and then it too would be flooded with gas just in case. There were emergency buttons near each person.

The cages where they rested were heavily padded, the material wrapping around them to prevent them from rolling over during the suspension. The major problem was that acceleration added to weight and a person who shifted around during the flight could break bones. They had to be held steady.

Jefferson left the bay and watched as one of the ship's medical staff checked the readouts on the bulkhead and then flooded the chamber with gas. Finally, the doctor turned and said, "You ready?"

"No," said Jefferson. "I hate this."

"Nothing to it. You go to sleep and when you wake up, you'll be at the destination."

"Shit."

"Hey, it's better than living for three weeks in a suit. Gets pretty ripe in there after three or four weeks. Can't scratch, can't wash, can't even have the luxury of taking a good healthy dump. Stuck with all sorts of tubes stuck in all sorts of uncomfortable places."

"I think it's a trade-off," said Jefferson.

"If you'll follow me."

Jefferson followed the man to a small chamber where the rest of his staff was already in suspension. He looked at the coffin-sized boxes, stacked up against one of the bulkheads, and remembered pictures he'd seen of the Vietnam War. Metal boxes holding the bodies of men killed in the war. That picture was suddenly superimposed on the scene in front of him.

"Shit," he said again, under his breath.

"Colonel?"

Jefferson turned and looked at the man but had nothing to say to him. He entered the bay and found his box. He crawled in, made sure the connections were tight, and then lowered the lid. He reached down to where the emergency buttons were and stroked them with his fingers. Feeling them made him feel better.

Then, looking up at the lid of the box, no more than three inches from his face, he felt panic bubbling through him.

Suddenly he had to get out. He could stand it no longer. With his right hand he reached up to push on the lid, but as he did, a calmness washed over him. He closed his eyes for a moment, feeling free. And before he knew it, he was unconscious and the ship was accelerating through deep space.

7

JEFFERSON RAISED HIS hand to push on the top of the box, needing to get out and knowing that he couldn't. He waited for the gases to take over, to smooth out the mental bumps, to calm him, but the gases didn't come. With panic burning and his stomach on fire, he shoved at the top of the box and was surprised as the lid suddenly flipped up and out of the way. Bright light, white light, flooded the interior and Jefferson sat up suddenly, gasping.

And then fell back, his head spinning. The lights flashed and he didn't know what was happening to him. There were hands reaching, grabbing at him, and lifting him.

"What?"

"Are you all right, Colonel?"

Jefferson blinked rapidly and felt cold sweat blossom on his forehead and drip down his face. "Fine. What happened?"

"We're coming out of suspension."

"Out?"

The man laughed at the disorientation. It was normal for a person not to realize that the suspension was over. The sleep was so deep that dreams were suppressed and the passage of time was not felt. It seemed, to the patient, that only a few minutes had gone by.

49

"Yes. Out. How are you feeling?"

Again Jefferson tried to sit. He glanced to the right and saw that the others were getting up. Torrence was on her feet, wobbling as a female medic supported her.

Jefferson started to climb out of the box, slipped, and then was helped. He stood there, feeling the black curtain coming down over his eyes, and staggered forward one step. Hands reached out to steady him.

"Thanks."

"You feeling better?"

Jefferson nodded and the hands released him. He turned and looked at Torrence. Her color was bad. He tried to grin at her but wasn't sure if he made it.

"Captain Clemens wants to see you as soon as you're ready."

"I'd like Major Torrence and Captain Carter there too."

"Both of them should be ready for a briefing at that time."

Jefferson looked at the young sailor. He didn't appear to be more than nineteen. There was a thin moustache on his upper lip that looked more like a lack of shaving than a serious attempt to grow a moustache.

"When will the rest of the regiment be brought up?"

"In the next twenty-four hours. If you'll follow me."

Jefferson stood there not moving. He didn't feel capable of walking. His knees felt weak and he was still light-headed. He glanced up at the clock over the hatch, and studied the ruby-colored numbers as they ticked off the seconds and slowly counted off the minutes.

Finally he felt good enough to walk. He moved closer to the young man and said, "What about a chance to clean up. Toilet. Brush my teeth."

"On our way to see the captain."

"We in orbit yet?"

"Captain'll tell you all that you want to know about all that."

They left the bay, moved through the dimly lit corridors telling Jefferson that it was night on the ship. They reached his quarters and the young sailor stayed outside while Jefferson went in. A clean uniform was hung over the back of the chair. In the alcove, he found a clean towel, soap, and everything else he would need. He took a long shower, knowing that the water that was pouring on him was the same that had gone down the drain moments before.

Finished with that he shaved, cutting away the sparse stubble that was all that had grown during the suspension. He looked at his fingernails but they hadn't seemed to grow and his hair didn't look that much longer. He stood there, studying his reflection in the mirror, staring at it but not really seeing it. His mind had stopped functioning for the moment. His image slipped out of focus and then slowly came back in.

The knocking at the hatch caught his attention. "I'll be finished in a moment," he yelled.

Naked, he walked to the chair and slowly dressed. He sat down in the chair and took several deep breaths. The after-effects of the suspension were supposed to wear off quickly but they hung on confusing him.

Finally he stood up and walked to the hatch, opened it, and joined the sailor in the corridor. When they reached the bridge, Torrence and Carter were already there. Both looked to have recovered from the suspension quicker. They looked alive. Jefferson felt half dead.

As soon as he walked in, the screen flickered and changed. Now most of it was taken up with a blue-green planet, part of the surface obscured by bright clouds.

"As you can see," said the captain. "We have arrived."

"Tactical situation?" asked Jefferson, his brain slowly beginning to function.

"Five of our outposts have refused to answer our calls. Two still have emergency messages broadcasting. Sensor probes suggest that all seven of the camps are deserted. There are readings indicative of the colonists still being there."

"Meaning?" asked Torrence.

"They're dead," said the captain. "Organic signals suggest the decomposition of bodies."

"Christ," said Carter.

The view on the screen changed. Now it was a stylized map showing the human outposts on the planet. There was a large concentration of people near the shallow bay where the shuttles landed. It was a city of several thousand people whose whole lives were now geared to helping those who wanted something more to get out into the field.

Strung out over the plains of the continent were the human outposts looking like the oasis of an interstate highway system on the old Earth.

Captain Clemens told them that the last outpost to send out the emergency call was one of the those closest to the city. Again the sensor sweeps had revealed nothing of importance. They had done nothing except passive survey so that those on the ground had no idea that a fleet had arrived.

"I'd like to put a company down there," said Jefferson. "And I'd like to put another down at the first outpost attacked. Both forces could sweep toward each other and we'd have a large reserve to protect the city if that was necessary."

Carter asked, "Sensor probes reveal any enemy activity?"

"Signatures of the aliens aren't defined enough for us to tell them from the largest of the animals down there but we do know that there are no large concentrations of animals near any of the outposts."

"That raises another question," said Torrence. "Are there animals that we have to watch for? Anything dangerous to us?"

"There are two large, felinelike predators, both capable of killing a human, but there are no reports that either has ever attacked a human."

"Captain Carter, I expect you to prepare a full briefing on the local flora and fauna, available before planetfall," said Jefferson.

"Already in the works, Colonel."

Again Torrence asked a question. "Preliminary reports suggested a rudimentary spaceflight. Have we examined the other inhabited planet?"

"Not as yet. Our attention has been directed to our outposts. Diplomatic contact will be established just as soon as we can arrange it."

"We seem to be digressing here," said Jefferson. "What else can you tell me about what is going on down there?"

"Right now, nothing," said the captain. "The city, warned of some kind of hostile activity, is preparing for an attack. Local militia is training."

"Why didn't they send out a rescue force?"

Clemens shrugged. "It wasn't their job. It was ours. They're probably waiting for us to arrive before they venture out from the safety of their walled city."

"How do you know that?"

"It'd be SOP."

"They could have made some effort," said Jefferson.

"They are colonists and not soldiers."

Jefferson looked at Torrence and then Carter. "I'll want the both of you to get as much information as you can before planetfall."

"Which companies will you deploy?"

Jefferson looked at his exec. "Captain Sinclair's and Captain Jorgenson's. Both to be ready within twenty-four hours. And I'll want a battalion standing by for deployment into the city as the situation dictates. Major Torrence, you'll wait to deploy with the battalion. You'll go just as soon as we're down and have an airhead established."

"Yes, sir. Where will you be?"

"I'm going in with Captain Jorgenson's company. I want to get my feet on the ground."

"I'm not sure that's a good idea," said Clemens.

"I'm not interested in your opinions, Captain. I want to get a firsthand look at the situation on the ground and I can't do that while on the ship. Therefore, I will accompany a company on planetfall."

"That puts both you and your second in command off the ship at one time."

"You'll be here, and besides, we'll be in communications the whole time. It's nothing to worry about."

"SOP dictates that one of you should be on the ship at all times."

"Why? You're competent. You can handle the problems. Besides, the regiment is supposed to deploy to the planet's surface. The commander should lead his troops, not hang around on the fleet directing them from above."

"It's your call, Colonel," said the captain. "I just don't like it."

Jefferson turned his attention on Torrence. "I'll expect you to supervise the revival of the people of the deployment companies."

"Yes, sir."

"Carter, you remain here for a complete debriefing and then inform me of anything that I need to know."

"Yes, sir."

With that Jefferson walked back toward the elevator that would take him off the bridge. Torrence stood there dumbfounded and then hurried after him. As the doors slid open and they entered, she asked, "What in the hell is going on?"

"Nothing."

The doors closed and they were falling away from the bridge. Torrence faced him. "What in the hell is going on?" she asked again.

"What do you mean by that?"

She shook her head and hesitated as if trying to organize her thoughts. Finally she said, "I mean that you don't seem to be overly interested in what is going on around you."

"I listened to as much of that as I needed to. Captain Carter, as the intelligence officer, must listen to it. His job is to determine what I need to know and what I don't need to know. I don't need to know, for example, that there are two large predators on that planet."

"It is information that might save a life."

"And that's why Captain Carter is there to get a full briefing on it."

"I don't understand you," said Torrence. "One moment you've got your fingers in every pie and the next you're detailing important duties to your subordinates."

"You don't understand me!" shouted Jefferson. "You aren't required to understand me." He lowered his voice. "All you have to do is your job and that is to listen to me. You don't have to understand me."

"I merely meant . . ." started Torrence.

"I'm not interested in what you meant." Jefferson stared at her for a moment. "You have no concept about command."

"I commanded a company."

"That's not the same," said Jefferson. "With a company, and even a battalion, there is someone else there. Someone else over you. But here, with this regiment, it's just me. I make the decisions, right or wrong. No advice from higher headquarters because the higher headquarters is three hundred light-years away. Four, eight, ten weeks to get a response with a drone scout ship. I'm the ultimate authority with no one to answer to right now. I am king or God, or any other name you want to give me."

"Christ," she said, not realizing the irony of the statement.

"Command is something that no one understands until he or she has to face it. Everyone hates you for some reason. Maybe they think you're suddenly too important. Maybe they think you somehow got your position but didn't deserve it. Maybe they're all waiting for you to fall on your face so that they can point and claim they knew it was going to happen all the time."

"No one thinks that.

"Shit," said Jefferson. "I'm not stupid. I know that everyone on the staff still resents the way I was brought in and elevated over them."

"Apparently not everyone," said Torrence.

"Now what does that mean?"

"Seems that you and young Lieutenant Norris have gotten to be fast friends."

Jefferson wanted to reach out and slap her. He stood there, staring down at her but said nothing.

Torrence held up her hand and said, "I understand it. Everyone needs to talk to someone."

"It's not like that," said Jefferson.

Torrence realized that she was caught out in the field. Norris was the one thing that she shouldn't have mentioned. It was a private thing, between Jefferson and Norris. It was not something that they should talk about. It was personal business between the two officers.

Jefferson, on the other hand, suddenly had to talk about it. "She's not a line officer. I won't be ordering her into combat at any time. As the supply officer, she remains here, on the ship, safe. There is no favoritism operating there."

"You're supposed to talk to me," said Torrence. "That's part of my job."

"Let's just drop it," said Jefferson.

The doors opened then and they stepped out. Sinclair was standing in the corridor, looking as if she didn't have a clue about what was happening. Jefferson pointed at her. "Planetfall in twenty-four hours."

"We'll never get ready," she said automatically.

"We'd better," said Jefferson. "You'll have one company on the ground."

"Shit." she said.

"My feeling exactly."

8

WITH LESS THAN an hour to planetfall, Jefferson was sure that something important had been forgotten. Those who were awake had been working since the moment they had been pulled from sleep without a break except to eat a quick, cold meal. Equipment had to be taken out of storage, checked for damage, cleaned, and put into service. The medical staff had been checking everyone to make sure that all booster shots were current even though no one knew what sort of bacteria they might face. Humans had been living on the planet for years but anyone in a weakened state would be susceptible to infection.

The officers were cross-checking the deployment companies making sure that each of them had a full complement. Equipment was issued and then stored in the drop modules. Men and women worked around the clock trying to get everything ready, each of them aware of the minutes snapping off the clocks mounted on the bulkheads around them.

Torrence arrived and reported, "Sinclair's company is ready for deployment."

"She made good time."

"Yes, sir."

Jefferson said, "Have them standing by."

"Where will you be waiting, sir?"

Jefferson shrugged and then said, "In the drop bay with Jorgenson's company. Report their deployment."

"Yes, sir." She turned and trotted off.

Jefferson took a final look around the tiny room that served as his quarters and office. He touched a button clearing the screen and filing the letter on a diskette. If he was killed, when that information was added to the computer, his final will and testament would appear on the screen.

Satisfied, he grabbed a baseball-like hat and entered the corridor, moving toward the drop bay. He tried to remember everything that he had been told in the last twenty-four hours. The briefing that Carter had prepared had slipped by him. He could remember nothing of it, not that it mattered. The Command Module was set with a microcomputer that could retrieve the information if needed. And since the natives had spacetravel, even if it was limited, it opened up a wide variety of support capabilities for them including thermonuclear attack from orbiting platforms if they decided to try it.

He entered the drop bay. The deployment modules were sitting on the floor. They were set in platoon-sized rings, one pod for each of the soldiers. The command module contained five pods and there was a second command ring with ten. The pods would protect the soldiers as they ejected from two to three hundred thousand feet above the planet's surface and could put the whole company down within inches of a chosen landing site. The defense of the airhead could begin before the people ever popped out of the modules.

Jefferson hated being closed in the pod almost as much as he hated being sealed into the suspension chambers. It seemed there were always excuses for sealing him into something that was almost too small for him. They were always finding ways of making military duty abhorrent. Trying to take his mind off the latest trouble, he watched as the soldiers ran across the shuttle bay floor completing the final steps before deployment.

Jorgenson ran up, stopped, and saluted. He was a short, thin man with very black hair and very white skin. He had piercing blue eyes that seemed to mask the rest of his features. They blazed, drawing attention to them. It was only later that anyone noticed how white his skin was.

"Sir, happy to have you deploying with us." He snapped off the salute so sharply it looked as if he had dislocated his shoulder.

"Take it easy," said Jefferson, wondering if he had ever been that young or enthusiastic. Then it dawned on him that Jorgenson probably wasn't more than two or three years younger than him. It was the price of winning that damned medal. It threw everything out of whack.

"Yes, sir. I just wanted you to know what an honor this is."

"Yes. Thank you." He stared at the young man. "Isn't there something you need to be doing."

"Yes, sir."

As Jorgenson turned to run off, another shape approached him. The man didn't wear a uniform and carried no military equipment. For a moment Jefferson thought that it was another of the ship's crew and then he recognized Garvey. He carried a metal briefcase, wore an old army pistol belt complete with a combat knife and a canteen, and looked as if he was about to head out on safari in old Africa.

"Just what in the hell are you made up for?" asked Jefferson.

"Planetfall. I'm covering it."

"Oh, no, you're not," said Jefferson. "We don't have room for superfluous personnel."

"I've got a right to go down with you," said Garvey. "The general . . ."

"Isn't here. I am and I say that you're not going to deploy with us."

"Afraid that I'll see something that I'm not supposed to see?"

"No," said Jefferson. "There's nothing down there for you to see. I'm more concerned that you'll get yourself killed or that you'll get in our way as we're trying to do our jobs."

"I won't get in the way and if I do get killed, I'll be out of your hair forever."

"Oh, no," said Jefferson. "If you get killed I'll spend weeks writing reports about it. There'll be investigations and hearings and reviews. And when the Army gets done, there'll be civilian commissions to review the incident not to mention the continuous hassle thrown up by your employers. Everyone will want to know why we weren't more protective of our distinguished representative of the video industry. Even if you disobey orders, ignore advice, and do everything in your power to get yourself killed, they'll still blame me."

"But I'm going anyway," said Garvey.

Jefferson nodded slowly, dumbly, as if he was giving in and then suddenly stepped in close, his face only inches from Garvey's. With a stiffened index finger, Jefferson poked Garvey's chest. "You are only going if I decide to permit it. There is nothing you can do if I decide you're staying right here. My word is the law. It is the way things are going to be. Cross me and it's the end of you. Stay out of the way, don't make waves, and we'll get along fine."

"I won't compromise my integrity as a journalist," said Garvey.

Jefferson shook his head. "Did I ask you to compromise anything? No. Did I ask to review the stories you file? No. Did I say that you'll obey orders so that you don't get killed? Yes. I hope you understand the difference."

Garvey lifted up on his briefcase and adjusted his grip. He stared up into Jefferson's eyes, and then had to grin. "As long as we understand each other."

"As long as we understand that."

For a moment a silence hung between them, and then Garvey to fill the void said, "You know Custer had a reporter with him when he rode into the Little Big Horn."

"And the reporter, not listening to the sage advice of Custer's superiors, died along with five companies of the Seventh Cavalry."

"So the man provided a precedence for the both of us."

Jefferson tired of the discussion. "If there is an empty pod, you may deploy with us. If not, you'll have to wait for the resupply shuttle."

"That'll be fine."

Jefferson turned and yelled, "Jorgenson!"

The young officer ran back. "Yes, sir."

"Find a pod for *Mister* Garvey, but do not leave any of your personnel here to accommodate him."

"No problem, sir. We've a number of empty pods available."

"Great," said Jefferson.

One of the ship's company came up and said, "We're getting close to drop, sir."

Jefferson nodded. To those around him, he said, "Let's get to the pods."

"Sir," said the sailor, touching Garvey on the shoulder, "your case will have to be left behind."

"No. I have to take it with me."

"There is no room in the pod for it. Just weapons. Your case won't fit into the weapons slot."

"But I need it."

Jefferson said, "Can you get it into one of the equipment pods?"

"Yes, sir. I think so."

"Then do that." To Garvey he said, "We'll do all we can to get it back to you on the ground."

Garvey reluctantly released the case and then warned, "You'd better."

"We need to get everyone into their pods," said the sailor.

Jefferson turned and moved toward his. He looked at the company. Now they were nothing more than dull green painted pods. Human-sized beans that when split would produce a fully grown, armed adult. But right now, sitting under the unmerciful lights of the deployment bay, they looked harmless, almost peaceful. Nothing to indicate the deadly nature of them.

A sailor held open the pod. Jefferson turned and backed into it. The sailor slowly closed it and Jefferson heard the quiet clicks as it snapped shut. Now the inner glow came on. A pale blue-green light so that the person in the pod could see his surroundings. There were gauges in most of the pods so that the soldier would have something to watch while sealed inside. Everything about the deployment pod was automatic, but it was psychologically necessary for the soldiers to feel they had some kind of control over their destiny.

In Jefferson's pod, as in all the command pods, there were heads-up displays that provided a wide variety of data to the commander. He would know how many of the pods had deployed, the physical state of the soldiers in them, and the terrain below them. He could learn about the weather conditions, concentrations of the enemy, if the nature of the enemy had been determined, and if there were any large animals waiting. Almost everything he needed was provided on the heads-up. There was also a commo link in case that was needed.

Now, sealed inside the pod, afraid that it was going to become his coffin, Jefferson concentrated on the heads-up, watching the endless parade of information. Status reports on his company and on the other. Time checks, and instrument checks, and updated information. One pod suddenly went down and the heads-up told him the pod had failed, but the soldier had been taken from it safely. One fewer for the deployment. He wished it could have been Garvey.

And then realizing that he had been given an answer to the immediate problem, he opened the command circuit. "See that Mr. Garvey's pod fails."

"Yes, sir."

There was a hesitation and then the signal came up. Garvey's pod was down. Jefferson grinned to himself. Garvey would be madder than hell, but there wasn't a thing he could do about it. Later, he could come down on the shuttle, probably would, but by then, Jefferson would have an idea what was happening on the ground. It wouldn't be quite so dangerous.

There was then a quick countdown on his display screen. Numbers unrolling in front of his eyes, and finally a sudden, heavy pressure on his chest. He wanted to reach up and push the weight aside but his arms were leaden, trapped in the soft foam of the pod. Blood was pounding in his ears and he saw that his heart rate, respiration, and blood pressure were all elevated. Sweat blossomed, dripped, and dried. A cold sweat.

Then, as suddenly as it had come, the pressure was gone. It felt like the bottom had dropped out. His head spun and his stomach rotated as the sliding pressures, sensations, feelings shifted and changed. Sweat beaded and dripped and then seemed to freeze in place and he thought that he was going to be sick, just as he thought during all the other drops.

The display continued to show him what was happening around him, but he could no longer focus on it. The letters and numbers were nothing more than smears of color on the screen, the colors telling him something. He tried to focus on it but couldn't.

There was a flash and a quiet electronic voice warned him,

"Thirty seconds to ejection. Thirty seconds to ejection. Twenty-nine, twenty-eight, twenty-seven . . ."

Jefferson tried to put the insistent voice out of his mind. He tried to see the parading numbers and words but they were jumbles of color and nothing more. He took a deep breath and tried to concentrate but the electronic voice kept intruding with the countdown.

"Fifteen, fourteen, thirteen . . ."

Panic gripped him as it always did. Now he had to get out. He pushed against the lip of the pod but it didn't budge. He gritted his teeth, relaxed, and then, screaming, pushed at the lid. He groaned deeply, his muscles popping with the strain, but it was now too late.

"Three, two, one. Eject! Eject! Eject!"

And they were tumbling free of the shuttle, plunging down into the thickness of the planet's atmosphere. The pod buffeted as it struggled to right itself. There were slight vibrations as the pod fell.

Jefferson watched the numbers of the altimeter unwind. Watched as they fell through the air like an anvil, plummeting like a meteor.

There was a pop behind his head as the drag chute deployed. The numbers slowed from a blur and Jefferson focused his attention on them. He watched as they began to crawl and realized that they were now close to touchdown.

An instant later there was a light bump, a roll, and then nothing. They were down safely. The hatch clicked once and popped open and Jefferson rolled out, a weapon in his hand.

His first impression was of a hot, humid plain. Hot and humid compared to the controlled environment on the ship. A breeze blew, rattled the leaves in the distant trees. Green leaves on brown trees, just like those on Earth. Greens and browns and blacks with flashes of color from the small flowers.

Jorgenson appeared, sweat covering his face and staining the dark green jumpsuit he wore. "Company deployed."

Jefferson nodded and turned. The pods were scattered over the open plain that sloped gently down to a valley. In the distance were the remains of the stockade that had protected the camp.

"Enemy movement?" asked Jefferson. It was an unnecessary question because his heads-up had told him that there were no enemies around. No indications of concentration of any large animals.

"Nothing."

Jefferson nodded. "Get the people formed and ready to move out in twenty minutes."

"Guard for the pods?"

"A single squad should do it."

"Yes, sir." He hesitated and then asked, "What happened to the journalist."

"Pod went down with mechanical failure," said Jefferson.

"That was convenient," said Jorgenson.

He turned and worked then to get his people ready. They had spread out in a skirmish line facing down the slope, toward the remains of the human outpost. Jorgenson waved a hand and the soldiers started forward, heading toward the camp. Heading down to learn what had happened there.

9

REARDON DID NOT know that the rescue force had finally arrived and that it had landed on the surface of the planet. He didn't know that there were soldiers out searching for any survivors who might have escaped the massacres at the human outposts. All he knew was that if the aliens found him they would kill him as quickly as they could.

Crouching at the base of a huge tree, hidden in the shadows there, sweating in the humid air and breathing in the sweetness of the blossoms that dotted the bush no more than twelve feet away, he knew there was only one thing working for him. The aliens didn't torture their captives as humans sometimes did. They did not make captives live in fear, did not threaten them and then hurt them, keeping at the painful activity until the victim died. They killed quickly. As fast as they possibly could.

He'd seen that as they had swarmed over the walls of the camp. He'd watched as they burned down the others, shooting them as quickly as they could. He'd seen them walk up to wounded men and women and dispatch them with single, merciful shots to the head. He'd seen them hammer humans to the ground, hitting them until the man or woman was dead, and then running off to attack someone else. And once he'd gotten out of the camp, he'd seen them catch and kill some of the other survivors. Always it was quick.

But none of that was important now that he had escaped the massacre. He had to get moving again. He had to try to reach the city across the plains where there would be some safety. He stood up and began to move even though it was still light. He wanted to get to the very edge of the forest so that he would have all night to cross the open plains. He would have the cover of darkness so that it would be harder for the aliens to see him.

He worked his way through the forest, some of the undergrowth grabbing at his feet, trying to trip him. Sunlight streamed through the breaks in the canopy over him and he tried to avoid those. He wiped the sweat from his face and then licked it from his hand. He didn't like losing moisture because he'd have to replace it and that meant drinking the local water. In the months they'd been there, they'd never discovered anything wrong with the local water, but they had always treated it before releasing it into the community tanks. Now he had to drink it right out of the ground without the chemicals that would kill the foreign bacteria.

Movement to his right caught his attention. Movement in the shadows, almost seen, almost heard. A quiet scrambling as if someone was following him. It had been there in the past but when he'd tried to find it, tried to learn what was causing it, it somehow escaped him.

Reardon stopped moving and slipped to the ground. There was a thick carpet of leaves and needles and rotting vegetation that gave off a musky odor when disturbed. He lay there, the sweat drying, and listened, determined to find out who was stalking him. Patience, he decided, was the key. Patience.

So he lay there, and listened carefully until he heard the quiet scrape of a foot against the forest vegetation. A quiet rustling that wasn't caused by the light breeze, or the animals running through the tops of the trees.

Clutching the laser rifle that he had taken from the alien he killed, Reardon stood up slowly. He unfolded himself until he was upright and standing right next to a tree, deep in a shadow. He scanned the forest around him, searching for something that didn't belong there. Searching for something that had been following him.

Finally he saw movement. Just a flash of brightness against the darker background of the forest. Not a natural color like the plumage of a bird or the bright green of a lizard, but something more of an Earth tone, more of a flesh tone. Slowly, Reardon raised his rifle and aimed it in the general direction of the stalking alien.

The movement came again along with a flash of blond hair. Reardon dropped to one knee and lowered the rifle. He waited, heard a rustling to the right, and a woman burst out of the trees standing no more than twenty feet from him. A small woman, dressed in what had once been a jumpsuit but that had been reduced to little more than rags. Her hair was stringy and filthy and mud and dirt masked the features of her face. There was a black band of filth around her eyes that made her look like a raccoon.

It took her a moment and then she saw Reardon. One hand came up toward her mouth, and she said, "Oh."

Reardon didn't know what to do. He knelt, the laser in his hands, now pointed at the ground, and stared at the human wreck. She was bone-thin. The black at her eyes gave her face the look of a skull. She didn't seem to have the strength to stand, let alone move, but she had been following him for a long time.

"Who are you?" he asked.

She looked at him dumbly, like a dog who recognized its master's voice but couldn't comprehend the words. She cocked her head and didn't move.

"Come on," said Reardon.

But the woman didn't move. She was like a deer caught in the headlights of a car. Afraid to move. Unable to move. She looked as if she was about to turn and flee.

Reardon set the rifle on the ground near him and slowly pulled out the canteen that he had taken from the alien. He uncapped it and held it out, offering it to her. "Water," he said. "Would you like some water?"

That did the trick. She nodded once and then nearly leapt forward. She snagged the canteen in both hands and tilted it up, to her lips, drinking quickly. Water dribbled from the corners of her mouth, running down to the ripped collar of her jumpsuit.

When she finished, she handed it back. "Thanks."

"You're welcome." Reardon capped it and then looked up at her. "So you can talk."

"Of course."

Reardon took a deep breath and was going to ask her what she was doing running around the forests of a now hostile planet, but he knew the answer. It was the same thing that he was doing. Running from the aliens. Instead, he grinned at her, wished he had a chance to wash his face and comb his hair, and asked, "What's your name?"

Now she moved back, almost afraid. She watched him with large, doelike brown eyes. "Rachel."

"Well, Rachel, maybe we should travel together. What do you think?"

She didn't answer. She just nodded.

Reardon picked up his rifle and then pointed toward the edge of the forest. "That way. Come along."

She said nothing but she did follow.

Torrence crouched in the tall grass near the foot of the stockade, her rifle in her hands, and listened to the sounds coming from inside the wall. Quiet sounds that were like those made by equipment on automatic. Servos and electric motors and automatic warning systems. Nothing that was living and breathing.

Spread out behind her were the men and women of the company, each covering the others, waiting for the officers to make up their minds. Sinclair finally crawled over to where Torrence hid, sweat dripping to the dirt as the planet's sun beat down on them, feeling hotter than Earth's ever did.

"What are you going to do?" asked Sinclair.

"It's your company. What are you going to do?" Torrence responded.

"Move one platoon forward while the others remain in place to provide cover just in case."

"Good."

Sinclair crawled off to alert her troops and Torrence worked her way forward, through the grass until she was right at the base of the stockade. There she could see that there were no real signs of attack. The stockade didn't look as if it had been blasted. There were laser tracks burned in the grasses, black arcs that were just beginning to be grown over. But nothing that suggested that there had been an all-out assault on the camp.

She halted there, staring down, into the grass. There were a few brightly colored bugs. Little, multilegged creatures of red or green or yellow. They seemed to be afraid of nothing and that made her wonder if they weren't poisonous to anything that might try to eat them.

Sinclair got her people organized and the assault platoon was suddenly up and moving, a narrow line of soldiers, weapons held hip high and pointed at the human camp. They moved slowly, as if afraid that the automatic defensive system might suddenly open fire through the commo operator would have already broadcast the IFF, identify friend or foe, code to prevent that.

Torrence climbed to her feet and joined the line. She let one of the soldiers walk past her and then followed him. They reached the wall and there was no indication that the defensive system was going to engage them.

Sinclair held up a hand to stop them and then ordered, "First squad forward."

Twelve soldiers broke from the line and ran forward, throwing themselves at the base of the wall. Gates through the stockade were open. They hesitated and then one at a time entered the stockade.

Torrence cocked her head, listening to the intra-squad communications. No one was saying much, other than it looked as if there were no survivors. Bodies were scattered everywhere inside the compound. The squad checked the community center, the guard shack, and a couple of residences.

"This is three alpha," crackled the radio. "No one moving. Guard center clear."

"Computer and replay capabilities?" asked Sinclair using her commo.

"Computers have sustained damage. Might be superficial. Memory modules might be intact."

"Roger."

"Ah, six, I think it's clear now. The rest of the command can enter the compound."

"Roger."

Torrence stayed where she was, waiting. The rest of the company came up, out of the tall grass near the ditch, and as they did, she joined them. Holding her rifle at port arms, Torrence hit the stockade wall and glanced into the compound. There were bodies visible. Two or three of them, lying on the hard-packed ground, baking under the sun.

She dodged around the corner and found herself in the compound. During her various combat tours, she had seen other battlefields. Human beings ripped to pieces under the hammering of machine guns, or torn apart in anger by the enemy. But here, it seemed to be different. The bodies weren't ripped to pieces. They weren't torn apart.

Torrence crouched near the body of a woman clothed in a light shirt that came to mid-thigh. Obviously she had been awakened by the attack and had run out to help in the defense. A single hole, blackened by the beam of a laser, had pierced the side of her head. She had collapsed and rolled and had died.

But the amazing thing was that there wasn't the sign of another wound. There was no sign of predator damage. There was no signs of a blood lust. She was killed by the aliens and once dead they had no interest in her. Not like on Earth where the victors mutilated the dead, sometimes because of religious beliefs and sometimes just to get even with the enemy.

Here, they killed. They destroyed the equipment and then they got out. The woman still wore a wristwatch, the numbers flashing, counting off the seconds, minutes, and hours.

Torrence stood up and moved on in. She headed toward the guard shack. It was as described. The computer screens were smashed, and the keyboards were rubble, but the disk drives and the memory units seemed to be intact. The aliens hadn't known that the information was contained in the memory.

A man sat at the console and was studying it carefully. He turned, looked at her, and said, "I think we can salvage some of this."

"That going to tell us what happened?"

"Don't know, Major. If they keyed it into the memory and

onto the hard drive before the screen was smashed, maybe. Anything floating in the memory would be lost."

"Pull what you can and we'll get it up to the fleet. Maybe they can make something of it."

"Certainly, Major."

Sinclair entered. She glanced at the destruction in the shack. "How long to get it working?"

"If we can get a monitor down here and the software that I need downloaded, maybe within a couple of hours. The enemy didn't know what to ruin so most of the equipment's in pretty good shape."

"You have the defenses operating tonight? By dark?" asked Sinclair.

The man shrugged and unbuckled his pistol belt. He tugged at the zipper of his jumpsuit revealing the vest underneath it. It would stop bullets and absorb the energy of a beam weapon, at least for a couple of seconds. He wiped the sweat from his face.

"Possibly. It depends on what we can get down from the ship and how much help I can get."

"Who do you need?"

"Bonds would be good. Benedict too. Either one but both would be better. And you'd better get someone who knows about the weapons systems to look them over."

Sinclair turned to Torrence. "I think that we'll be better off holding here for the night. It's a good defensive position. Better than anything else we can find."

"I agree," said Torrence. "But I don't think we should rely on the computers to protect us."

"Neither do I. What I want to do is use it as a backup system. Just one more thing that we can do."

"Good." Torrence turned and stepped to the door. She looked out on the compound. It was evident that the colonists had been attacked, killed, and that the enemy had then gotten out. There was no evidence that anyone had survived the assault. She glanced at the man at the console. "There a roster of the people here?"

"I haven't found anything, but I would guess there is."

Sinclair asked, "What are you thinking?"

"I don't remember there ever being a case where the entire

side was wiped out with the possible exception of the Fetterman Massacre in old Wyoming on Earth."

"What about Custer?" asked Sinclair.

Torrence shrugged. "Couple of those people might have gotten away. Maybe, maybe not. Half of one company, supposedly riding to their deaths with Custer, straggled in during the next day of fighting. The point, however, is that someone might have gotten out as the defense collapsed."

"We've had no signals," said Sinclair.

"So they didn't get out with any equipment. If you've been on a site for six, eight, ten months and there had never been a problem with the natives, you wouldn't expect an attack. When it came, maybe all you could do was get out with the clothes on your back."

"Then we need to get search parties out."

"Right," said Torrence, "but not right this second. If there are survivors, they've spent three or four weeks outside. Another few hours isn't going to kill them."

Sinclair shifted her rifle from one hand to the other. She wiped her face and then sat back, leaning against the console. "Tomorrow then."

"Once we get settled in here," said Torrence. "Then we'll fan out searching."

Torrence stood in the door and looked out at the sun-drenched compound. It didn't make sense. Why would the natives suddenly turn hostile? Did the humans, assuming that things were the way they were on Earth, somehow offend the locals, causing the trouble.

She watched as the men and women of the company moved from structure to structure, searching for a clue as to why everyone was now dead. They found nothing except evidence that the enemy had been very thorough. They had moved through every house, every building, every structure, killing everyone they found. That done, they got the hell out.

"I don't understand this," said Sinclair, suddenly standing next to Torrence.

Torrence glanced to the right, at the other officer, and said, "Neither do I."

10

JEFFERSON WAITED AS the compound was explored and then entered it himself. Armed men and women were standing near the palisade, at the doors to residences, near the computer center, the power station, and the command post. Bodies of the dead, decaying, were scattered on the ground. The stench from them hung heavy in the air.

"Camp's clean," said Jorgenson. "No sign of the enemy. No survivors."

Jefferson wiped at his nose. The sickeningly sweet odor was beginning to affect him. "I want a graves registration detail to take care of this."

"We're going to need to identify the bodies," said Jorgenson.

"We're going to get sick if the problem isn't eliminated. Photographs and holos should be sufficient. I want the dead buried quickly. Before there is a chance for disease."

"Yes, sir."

Jefferson turned and glanced up, toward the sun and then back down at the camp. No evidence that the enemy had blown their way into the compound. No evidence of an attack on the outside. All the damage and the dead were on the inside.

"Computers?" asked Jefferson.

"We're checking on that. I'll let you know something as soon as possible."

"I want our base set up outside the walls."

"Why?" asked Jorgenson. "This is a good defensive perimeter."

"Except it did nothing for the people who were here. The enemy breached the walls with ease. Besides, there is a real concern about disease."

"Yes, sir."

Jefferson shot a glance at the younger officer. "And we don't need sarcasm. You have your orders. Watch the smart aleck tones."

"Yes, sir."

"And then I want an up-link with the ship as soon as it can be arranged."

Jorgenson nodded and said, "Yes, sir." He turned and trotted off to arrange it.

Jefferson stood there for a moment. The interior of the camp looked like no battlefield he'd ever seen. There were bodies of the dead, but they hadn't been mutilated. Most of the equipment was right where it had been dropped. And there were no enemy dead. Jefferson was convinced there should have been some, and he figured that the enemy had carried the bodies away.

A soldier approached, saluted, and said, "We've got up-link with the fleet."

"Thanks." Jefferson followed the woman back, toward what had been the command post. The interior was ruined. The equipment had been smashed, the bits and pieces of it littering the hard plastic floor. It crunched underfoot.

The walls showed some signs of fighting. Scorch marks on them and on some of the equipment. An electrical fire that had been suppressed by the chemical retardants sprayed on it. And a single, fist-sized hole punched through the plastic wall, the edges blackened by the beam that had done it.

One of Jefferson's soldiers sat at the console, one of their own comms sitting on top of it. It had been plugged into the compound's main power feed.

"You have power?" asked Jefferson.

"Nothing wrong with the generating station, sir," said the

man. "It apparently shut down automatically with only superficial damage. We repaired it in five minutes."

Jefferson sat down and looked at the blank screen. The man reached over and touched a button. The captain's face appeared. He said, "Ready, Colonel."

"Captain Clemens," said Jefferson, "first, I want a status report on the other landing party."

"Down and inside the compound. No enemy contact and no sign of survivors."

"Scanners and sensor report?"

"We've located nothing of importance. We've recalibrated in an attempt to find any single humans outside those compounds, but the sweeps take time. Vegetation can mask the sweeps."

"Keep at it," said Jefferson unnecessarily.

"Yes, sir."

"Enemy situation?"

"Negative as far as we can tell. Nothing from their cities either on their home world or here to suggest a state of war exists. Nothing to indicate large groups of them on the march, and nothing that would suggest any of them around our remaining outposts."

"I take it those have been apprised of our findings here."

"Yes, sir, but the leadership there doesn't see what that has to do with them. They say they have the defense in the cities even if the outposts can't. They claim they are safe right where they are and are not going to be panicked from their homes."

"Anything else?"

"I had a visit from your journalist friend. He has requested immediate transportation to the planet's surface."

"I hope you informed him that we are not in the habit of running a personal taxi service and that he'll have to wait until accommodations can be made."

"Yes, sir."

"Now. Anything else?"

"No, sir. We're standing by, waiting for further instructions."

"I want the one battalion equipped and ready to launch on fifteen minutes' notice. Do not advise Mr. Garvey of that

situation. I want the scouts out now with a report to me in thirty
minutes. And I want this up-link open at all times."

"Understood."

Jefferson glanced at the people near him and then back at the
screen. "That's it for now." He stood up and one of the
operators slipped into the chair he had abandoned.

Without a word to anyone else, Jefferson moved out into the
compound. Jorgenson had already started clearing the area of
the dead. A detail was photographing the bodies with both
holographic and film cameras. A group of people, wearing gas
masks, were loading those already processed into plastic bags.

Jorgenson appeared then. "Under way, sir."

"Good. Do you have a patrol out searching for a campsite
for us?"

"Yes, sir. They've reported a ridge to the west that looks
promising."

Jefferson stood there, sweating in the blazing sun, uncomfortable under the weight of his uniform shirt and the bulletproof, laser-absorbing vest he wore under it.

"Tomorrow," he said, "we begin patrolling the surrounding
countryside."

"Yes, sir." Jorgenson didn't sound as if he relished the idea.

They moved through the day, sticking to the shadows and the
deepest parts of the forest. They didn't talk, the woman
following Reardon wherever he might be taking her. She didn't
care, as long as she was with another human. It had been a long
time since she had seen a living person.

Reardon had tried to get her to talk more, as they pushed on,
but her failure to respond or her noncommittal answers soon
discouraged him. He knew, just because it had happened to
him, that she had escaped a massacre. There was no other
reason for the woman to be alone in the woods.

Reardon stopped once and then knelt near the end of a
rotting log. Through a gap in the vegetation, he could look out
over a large, empty field. On Earth, it might have belonged to
a farmer who had prepared it for planting. The dirt had been
scraped clear of vegetation and then cultivated, turning the soil
over so that it was softer and would retain the rain. The field
came up to the edge of the forest and then stopped, almost as

if the trees had provided a barrier that the farmer could not penetrate.

He turned and looked at the woman. She was staring out but said nothing. Reardon turned his attention back to the field and waited. After several minutes, he was certain that no one, or no alien, was about to return. He sat down then, took out his canteen, and drank from it.

"Do you mind?" she asked, holding out a hand.

Reardon looked at her and then shrugged. "There isn't much left."

"I'll be careful." She tilted the canteen to her lips and drank. Finished, she handed it back.

Reardon took it and capped it. He then held a hand up to his eyes and looked upward, into the sky. "We've about three hours of daylight left."

She didn't respond to that.

"I figure we can cover another couple of kilometers in that time. Get closer to the coast."

"That your destination?"

"Of course. Isn't it yours?"

Now she shrugged as if to say that it made no difference one way or the other.

Reardon wiped the sweat from his face and took a deep breath. Slowly, he climbed to his feet. "If you're ready, we'll get going."

He didn't wait for her to say a word. Instead he turned and pushed his way into the vegetation, ducking under a low-hanging limb. He stopped once, close to what looked like a spiderweb. That was something he hadn't seen before and he was curious about it until the web's owner appeared.

Reardon jumped back and then slipped off to the right, keeping his eyes on the black creature. It looked like a small squirrel with a large, hairy head and four eyes in a line across its face. The mouth was open and there were sharp teeth showing. The beast didn't seem to be afraid of Reardon, even though he was so much larger than it.

Rachel stood there for a moment, fascinated by the animal. It seemed to watch her, its head and eyes on her as it slowly inched its way along the top of the web. Given the size of it,

Reardon was sure that it weighed a couple of pounds, which meant the web was very strong.

"Let's go," he said.

And as he spoke, the creature leapt. The two front feet, looking like the paws of a squirrel, were outstretched, the little fingers pointed at Rachel. It hit her in the chest and she screamed, a single, high-pitched shriek.

Reardon jumped toward her as she fell back. She reached up and grabbed the beast near the throat, holding it away from her face. The teeth flashed as it tried to bite her neck. The little hands clawed at her flesh, ripping it and leaving short, bloody wounds.

"Get it off! Get it off!"

Reardon stood there for a moment, unsure of what to do. He didn't want to touch the beast. He was slightly afraid of it. And his weapon was useless. The thing was too small. He'd probably hit the woman instead.

"Help me. *Get it off!*"

Reardon crouched and set his weapon down. He reached out, froze, and then straightened. Rachel was kicking now, her feet drumming on the soft carpet of dying vegetation. She was rolling right and then left, lying on her back, screaming.

Reardon finally snaked a hand out. He touched the stiff fur of the creature. Its head swiveled and snapped at him once, and then it tried to sink its teeth into the woman. Reardon grabbed it then, right behind the head. Squeezing, he pulled at it. The woman released it and it tried to turn to attack him. Now the beast was shrieking, squirming, trying to rip into Reardon's hand and arm.

Reardon stood and whirled. Without thinking, he hurled the beast at the trunk of a tree. It hit with a quiet thud and fell to the ground. It didn't move again.

Reardon crouched over the woman. "You okay?"

She sat up and looked at the cuts on her hands. "Stings. Stings bad."

"You okay?"

She looked up at him and finally nodded. "I'm fine." She held up her hands and examined the wounds on them.

Reardon opened his canteen. "Here," he said, taking one of her hands. He poured some water on it.

"Don't waste it," she said.

"Doesn't matter now. The water's right up out of the ground. I've nothing to treat the water with. We can refill the canteen anywhere."

She shrugged as Reardon continued to wash her wounds. Finished, he asked, "You feel anything?"

"Stings. That's all."

Reardon looked over at the body of the beast. "Don't think anyone has cataloged that one yet." He helped her to her feet and then moved toward the web. He bent close but didn't touch it.

"I want to thank you," she said.

"No problem."

"Do we have much farther to go tonight?"

Now Reardon turned so that he could look at her. "I think we'd better get away from here. We made quite a lot of noise. Someone or something might have heard." He took her hands in his and looked at them. The scratches were deep and long, but little more than scratches. They were no longer bleeding.

"How far?" she asked again.

"How ever far we get," said Reardon. He let go of her hands and turned so that he could look at the animal again. He moved toward it and crouched near it. He didn't touch it again.

"What?" she asked.

"Nothing. Strange that a little animal would not be afraid of something so much larger than it."

"Snakes aren't afraid of people."

Reardon shrugged but didn't say that most of those unafraid were the ones that were deadly. Few small animals ventured out to attack and wouldn't fight unless cornered.

He ignored her and asked, "You ready to go?"

"Sure."

He looked at her carefully but she didn't look to be sick. Her skin color was good. There was sweat on her face and soaking the remnants of her jumpsuit but that was from the exertion and not poison.

"We'll go another klick or two," he said. "Then we'll look for a place to hole up for the night."

"Good," she said. She looked into his eyes and smiled for the first time. "I'll be glad when this is over."

"So will I," said Reardon. With that, he turned and pressed forward, into the forest. He hoped that she wasn't about to get sick. He hoped that the beast hadn't been venomous, but all he could do was hope for the best. And recently that hadn't been very good.

11

THE REPAIRED COMPUTER system displayed nothing. The automatic targeting system did not suddenly activate. There were no indications that anything was about to happen.

Torrence was standing at the door of the command center, looking out into the compound. She held her rifle in her left hand. The zipper of her jumpsuit was pulled down revealing part of the vest she wore. Sweat from the high humidity stood on her forehead, upper lip, and soaked the armpits and back of her clothes.

Sinclair strolled up, stopped, and then looked up at the night sky. "Stars look weird. None of the constellations are there."

"Constellations are just pictures made up by people," said Torrence.

"But with them missing from the sky, it shows how far we are from home."

"So what?"

"Christ, what's your problem?"

Torrence continued to stare. Finally she shrugged. "I don't know. This doesn't feel right."

Sinclair shifted her weapon to her right hand and held it up. "What doesn't feel right?"

"That's what I don't know," said Torrence. "The enemy

burst into here without tripping any of the automatic systems. Anything larger than a rabbit should be seen and challenged. Nothing should be able to get through, yet the attackers did."

"We don't know that," said Sinclair. "Computer records aren't complete."

Torrence turned and looked at her. "It's fairly obvious that the enemy got in here and killed everyone. And it's fairly obvious that no one was targeted outside the camp. No evidence of firing outside the wall."

"We're soldiers, not colonists," said Sinclair.

"Sometimes that's not enough."

"Shit," said Sinclair. She was beginning to feel anxious and she didn't know why. She glanced around, at the others who had come out into the open, at the walls, and finally over her shoulder into the command center.

"You've got pickets out?"

"In commo contact with us. That's one thing the colonists didn't have."

"Up-link with the fleet?"

"Established. No problems there."

And then, almost as if to prove Sinclair a liar, one of the men came out of the command center. "We've lost communications with the fleet."

Sinclair whirled. "What?"

"It's only temporary. Some sort of electromagnetic interference on a very low level. We'll have it corrected in a few moments."

"The pickets?"

"They're not to report in for another fifteen, twenty minutes," he said.

"Do it now," snapped Sinclair. "Right now."

"Yes, ma'am." The soldier spun and rushed back into the building.

"I don't like this," said Torrence.

"I wish you'd quit saying that. Just shut up."

Torrence watched as two men ran across the compound toward one of the gates, but then stopped short of it. Both men were confused. They stood there, looking at each other and then at the gate, but neither reacted.

"Go to full alert," said Torrence.

"Why?"

"Because I said to," she said. "That's all you need. A lawful order."

Sinclair didn't move for a moment and then nodded. She turned and stepped into the command center. Torrence watched her and then moved out into the middle of the compound. She now held her rifle in both hands, waiting.

"Someone's coming up on the north side," yelled a woman. "Ten, twelve, twenty of them."

Torrence turned, stared, and then ran back across the open ground. She stopped short, near the door of the command center, listening to the sounds growing around her. Shouts of the men and women on guard. Rustling as they ran to their posts, but no firing yet.

She entered the command center. The bank of screens that had shown the country around the camp were all snow-filled. A few ghostly images swayed on two of the screens but the interference was so bad that no one could tell if there was anything of significance displayed.

"What the hell?"

"Some kind of jamming," said Sinclair.

Torrence stood flatfooted in the bright lights of the command center, looking first at the screens and then out the door.

"Commo with the pickets?"

"Nothing."

Then from outside came the warning. "Here they come!"

Torrence whirled and rushed out. She hesitated, looking for the beginning of the fight. From the direction of the command center she heard shouting and then the defensive lasers began to shoot. Flashes of bright light strobing into the darkness. And just as quickly, the lasers failed.

Torrence ran to the north wall, climbed the steps up to the parapet, and looked over the top. The enemy, the creatures, were rushing forward. It was the first look at them that Torrence had gotten. The first time she'd seen any of them alive. Before, everything had been holos or pictures.

Around her, the soldiers began to fire. Lasers flashed again. Ruby-colored beams of light looking like the tracers seen in old war films. The creatures were hit, some of them falling but the others coming on.

Torrence raised her own weapon, aimed, and fired once. The pencil-thin beam flared and then vanished. The trunk of a small bush burst into a flame that died quickly.

Firing erupted from the onrushing enemy. Muzzle flashes strobed and bullets slammed into the wood of the palisade. There was a hammering of machine guns and the ground in front of her flashed and strobed until all motion on it looked like an old movie played through a faulty projector.

Dozens of the alien beasts were hit and fell. But hundreds more rushed from the cover of the forest or up out of the ditch that surrounded the camp. They were a silent group, with only a few of the weapons firing. Sporadic sounds that built and faded and then came back.

Around her, Torrence's own soldiers were falling. One hit in the head did a back flip off the parapet. Another was hit in the arm. She dropped her weapon and spun to the right, a hand on her shoulder. She sat down, looked at the blood smeared on her hand, and then passed out, falling to her side.

The creatures reached the base of the wall. They huddled there, like people trying to get out of a heavy rain. The palisade had not been built with a thought to an armed enemy reaching the base of it. There were no firing ports. To shoot down at the enemy, the men or women had to stand and lean over the top. That exposed them to the creatures firing up from the darkness below.

Torrence realized that she could do nothing on the parapet. One more rifle, more or less, would not change the outcome. She turned and ran along it, head bowed and shoulders hunched. At the stairs, she hesitated and looked back.

The firing was getting heavier. It was a strange, silent battle. Lasers flashing brightly. Beams of light crisscrossing in the air. Red light and green light. There were bursts of flame where the beams touched wood or cloth or the vegetation.

Torrence ran down the steps and headed toward the command center. She burst in and yelled, "Get an up-link with the fleet. Now."

"Commo is out," said the man, sounding as if nothing was wrong.

"That wasn't a request. It was an order. I don't care what you have to do to establish it."

The man's face paled slightly. He turned to the commo unit and touched the buttons. The tiny screen glowed green and then swirled with color. Nothing appeared on it.

"Link's down," he said.

Torrence stepped closer and lowered her voice. From outside came the hammering of old-fashioned weapons. Machine guns and automatic rifles. There was a popping. Flares fired and burst, some of them bright green or red that lasted for five or ten seconds and others hanging under parachutes.

"You work to get it restored and then you request immediate close air support. You request shuttles and you tell them that we have wounded. The situation could easily get out of hand."

"But that's impossible."

"And there shouldn't be aliens coming over the top of the palisade, but they are. Now you do it."

Before he could answer, she had turned and was out the door. To the right she could see one of the creatures. Six feet tall with a barrel chest and the pointed head that looked like an old-fashioned artillery shell. She aimed at the creature and fired. The beam struck it at mid-chest, seared a hole in it that flared as the cloth caught fire. The enemy dropped its weapon, lifted its hands to the wound, and then roared as it collapsed to the ground.

Sinclair was suddenly beside her. "Too many of them coming too fast."

"We've no commo with the fleet."

Sinclair shook her head. "So what are we going to do?"

"Abandon the walls and pick them off as they come over. We've already got some in the compound."

Sinclair nodded and sprinted away. Torrence glanced around but there was no cover available. The best place for her was right where she was. Near the command center where she could communicate with the fleet if that was needed. When the link was reestablished.

Retreating to the doorway, she crouched there, rifle in her hand. Across the compound, on the east wall, she saw one of the alien creatures. She aimed, fired, and missed. The enemy dived to the right and then rolled off the parapet. Again she fired. This time the creature was hit in the shoulder. It stood up and then fell, losing its weapon. As it searched the ground around it, she fired again, killing it.

Now the battle broke down into individual combat. Soldiers fighting with the aliens. Lasers against old-fashioned rifles. Clubs against razor-sharp knives. Hand against hand, though the soldiers didn't do well with that. The aliens were too big and too strong.

Torrence stayed where she was, searching for targets. A running alien that had just entered. Another standing on the parapet as if confused. A third firing at a soldier. And then a fourth coming at her, head down, as it fired again and again. Torrence killed it easily.

As the last creature dropped, Torrence glanced to the rear. "You got a linkup?"

"Close."

"Get it established, fuck face." She whirled as two aliens burst through the gate forty feet away. One turned right, running along the wall, firing as it ran. The other came at Torrence. It was growling from deep in its throat. It sounded like an angry freight train coming at her. As it raised its weapon, Torrence fired, but her shot was wide. The creature returned fire, but the slugs slammed into the plastic of the door frame.

Torrence dived to the right and rolled away. As she came up, the creature reached the command center and fired through the open door. The rounds disappeared inside. Torrence shot at it. The beam hit it low, near the knee, but the creature ignored that. It poured more rounds into the command center until Torrence killed it with a shot to the head.

As she stood up, she noticed that the firing was tapering. Fewer of the creatures were running around the interior of the compound. Firing was coming from the colonists' quarters, from the community buildings, from behind everything that could be used as cover. A deadly crossfire ripped into the alien ranks, chopping them down.

There was a sudden, piercing shriek and the attack was abandoned. One moment the compound was full of firing and the next the creatures were scrambling to get out. Lasers still flashed and the aliens still died.

Torrence stood up, sweat dripping from her face and trickling down her body. Suddenly she was aware of that, and the odors around her. Burnt flesh and hot copper. And the noise. Or rather the lack of it. Lasers didn't make noise when they fired. The people screamed and cursed, but it wasn't at the volume she'd expected. Single curses and quiet shouts.

Sinclair was suddenly near her again. "They're on the run now."

"Casualties?"

"I haven't had a chance to make a count. I think they're going to be heavy."

Torrence looked at the corpse-strewn compound. Some of the dead were obviously human and some were not and others couldn't be identified yet.

"Orders?" asked Sinclair.

"I want contact established with the pickets."

"I think they're all dead."

"Then find out." She took a deep breath and wiped her face. She glanced back into the command center. One of the men was lying on the floor, obviously dead. There was a pool of blood around him so that it looked as if he floated in it. The commo equipment was shot to pieces, smoke pouring from one of the consoles.

"Damage?" asked Torrence.

The other soldier who was crouched in the corner, a hand on her knee that was stained with blood, said, "I think everything is off the air."

Torrence looked at her. "You hurt bad?"

"Not as bad as Jerry. He's dead."

"Can you try to reestablish contact with the fleet. We need some help in here now."

The woman moved, groaned in pain as her face turned a pasty white. She reached out with a hand to steady herself and then stood up. "I'll do what I can."

Torrence turned back and looked out into the compound. There were small fires burning everywhere. Smoke poured from one of the residences and the automatic sprinklers were trying to fight it. There was a quiet hissing from it, barely audible above the other noises in the camp.

Sinclair said, "I think we've got fourteen dead and twenty-seven wounded."

"We'll get shuttles in to solve that problem."

"We've got commo with the fleet," said the woman.

Torrence spun and looked into the command center. The woman was sitting in front of the portable, the screen there now was clear. Those of the defensive console that hadn't been destroyed by rifle fire glowed. On one of them she could see the area just outside the north wall. It was littered with dead aliens, killed either during the attack or the retreat.

As she watched, the face of the captain appeared on the screen. He was sitting in his chair on the bridge, waiting for her to say something. Then, just as suddenly, that screen went blank.

"It's them, not us," she said.

"Christ," said Torrence. "Get them back."

The woman bent back to work, studying the tiny screen in front of her. Finally she turned. "We'll have to wait for them."

"Then get me Colonel Jefferson."

"I'll need a boost from the fleet to do it. Or get an antenna rigged down here."

Torrence just shook her head. The aliens were not supposed to be able to launch a sneak attack. The communication with the fleet was supposed to be permanent. And they were supposed to be able to contact the other landing team at all times. Everything was supposed to work and to work well. It had been tested. Repeatedly.

To Sinclair, Torrence said, "This isn't supposed to happen."

"So now what do we do?"

Not understanding the term because she'd never seen a football game but using it anyway, she said, "We drop back and punt."

12

"SIR, I'VE GOT a low-level electromagnetic band near one of the landing sites."

Clemens, sitting on the bridge, turned toward the woman and ordered, "Explain."

"It's masking all communications from the surface at the moment."

"Source."

"I'm not sure, Captain. It's a blanket broadcast and it's suppressing all communications and telemetry from one of the camps."

"Put it up on the screen," he said and then turned to face forward.

A map appeared, more of an aerial photograph, with terrain features and points of interest marked. It showed Jefferson's landing site in the lower left-hand corner and Torrence's in the center of it. Across the center, covering the location of Torrence's camp, was a broad red band indicating the area of interference. It was a bubble-shaped blotch.

"That natural or artificial?"

The woman shook her head. "Can't say yet. That activity came up slowly and is now pulsating."

"Eliminate it," said Clemens.

"I can't, sir. It's across the broadcast spectrum at a very low level. Just enough to disrupt our communications."

Now another woman spoke up. "Captain, I'm getting signs of unusual activity near the alien city on the sea. There are sources of electromagnetic radiation and we've been swept by radar."

"Only radar?"

"Yes, sir. Primitive broadband sweeps but the signal strength is enough to paint us on their scopes."

Clemens spun around to examine the screen. Since there were no distress calls from the surface using either the communications setup of the colonists or the up-link capabilities of the landing party, he assumed that nothing was wrong. Just some kind of low-level interference.

Jenkins, the woman who had made the first report, sat quietly studying her screen and the data readouts that paraded up her terminal. Using a keypad to the right, she changed the settings and tried to break through the electromagnetic pulsing. Nothing she did reduced the interference. It stayed at the same level, blocking all attempts at communication.

Now Jenkins turned to face the captain. "Sir, I am unable to penetrate the screening."

"Is there something there for us to concern ourselves with?"

"According to the intelligence briefings, the indigenous local personnel do not have the sophistication to block our transmissions across the entire spectrum. Therefore the problem must be a natural phenomenon and of no interest to us."

Clemens nodded. He turned to the other woman and said, "Give me a view of the land mass near the radar station."

"Yes, sir."

The view on the screen shimmered and shifted and swirled in bright colors, finally solidifying. Now there was a view of a land mass that was mostly flat. The upper right corner showed the beginning of the oceans.

"Radar site is marked in bright red. Military complexes are shown in yellow and sites of indigenous inhabitation are in green."

"Any human outposts visible?"

"No, sir. Closest human location is some four hundred kilometers to the north and out of view."

Clemens sat there for a moment watching the screen. There was nothing unusual on it. Alien, enemy locations marked, but there was nothing to indicate hostility. Even though the locals had spaceflight, it was interplanetary instead of interstellar. Launch of their manned vehicles was easily detected and it would be twenty-four hours before their craft could reach the fleet. There was nothing to worry about.

For several minutes Clemens sat there quietly, listening to the quiet noise of the bridge around him. The hums of the instruments, the pinging of the various sensors, and the rasp of radio and down-link commo. Some of the crew were talking, sharing information as more of it came in. Nothing unusual at all.

Then Jenkins broke the quiet. "I have commo established with Major Torrence on the ground."

Clemens ordered, "Put it on the main screen."

He saw the inside of the command center on the ground. It looked as if the interior had been shot up, but he didn't know if the damage was recent or if it had happened when the camp was destroyed earlier. Torrence appeared looking miserable. Her uniform was dirty, torn, and sweat-soaked.

Then, without warning, the scene shifted and buzzed and began to pulsate. A quiet voice repeated, "Missile launch. Missile launch. Missile launch."

"Tell me what's happening," said Clemens.

"There is multiple missile launch from near the radar site. Spread of twelve missiles coming up at us. Impact in twenty minutes."

"I thought someone said that we'd have twenty-four hours."

"That was a manned flight. These are unmanned missiles."

"We have a reading on the payload."

"Thermonuclear devices in the one to two megaton range," said a male voice from behind him.

"Course plot."

The screen changed again now showing the enemy missiles on one side and the fleet on the other. Red lines were drawn between the two showing that the missiles were on a collision course with the fleet.

"Helm, prepare to break orbit."

"Helm ready."

"I want a course reversal to break orbit." Clemens glanced down at the small screen near his left hand. "Plot us away from the planet and in toward their star. See if that'll mask our position."

"Course plotted."

"Weapons, target the incoming missiles now."

"Missiles targeted and ready to fire."

"Fire."

On the screen, the incoming missiles flared brightly and disappeared from sight. The red lines that had been drawn between the fleet and the missiles faded away.

"Prepare for shock wave."

"We've missile detection, Captain."

"Coming up?"

"No, sir. I've just got them plotted on my instruments. Now. Missile launch. I've one, two, three. They've launched twenty or more."

The shock wave hit them and then was beyond them. Some of the instruments registered increased radiation and heat. The flashes of light didn't bother them.

"Targeting?"

"We've got them."

"Helm, initiate the course change."

"Aye, sir."

"Targeting, you have permission to fire as soon as the missiles are in range."

"Aye, sir."

Clemens turned again and stared at the screen. It showed the missiles coming up at him. As before they were on one side with his fleet represented on the other.

"Missile launch," said Williams. "I now have an additional twelve missiles coming up."

"I've got a fleet detection," said Jenkins. "Two, three ships standing off five thousand kilometers."

"Class of the ships?"

"Unknown, Captain."

"Helm."

"Ready."

"Initiate the change."

There was a rumbling deep inside the ship but no sensation

of motion. The picture on the screen changed as the fleet began withdrawing. The gaps between the missiles and the fleet continued to narrow but not nearly at the rate it had.

And then the weapons officer opened fire again. There was no sound from the firing, no recoil from the weapons. He pushed a button, the weapon fired, and a missile vanished in a burst of heat, light, and radiation. One by one the missiles on the screen vanished.

"Unidentified ships are turning with us, Captain."

"Any hostile intent?"

"Negative, sir. They're mirroring our movements and staying at five thousand kilometers."

Glancing back at the screen, Clemens noticed that all the enemy missiles were gone. Vaporized by his weapons and the detonation of their own warheads.

Clemens was suddenly uncomfortable. Sweat beaded on his forehead and dripped. He wiped it away and then turned, looking at the men and women on the bridge. Most were staring into screens or instruments, looking for a clue about the enemy's intentions.

Finally he leaned back. Enemy missiles were still lifting, but now he was far enough away that he had an hour to target them. Those unidentified ships seemed to be interested in staying five thousand kilometers away.

"Damage reports?"

"None coming in, Captain. Elevated radiation counts. Interior heat up four point three degrees but has leveled off."

Clemens turned back to the screen but there was nothing on it to watch. The missiles were gone and the unidentified ships had slipped to seven thousand kilometers.

"We have an identity on those ships?"

"Negative, Captain. All I can tell you is that they're not part of our fleet and they are not part of an ally's fleet. Ship configuration, size, and weapons are unusual and most closely resemble those of the European Economic Community."

"Are you suggesting that they are from Euro-Econ?

"No, sir. I merely said they resembled the ships of Euro-Econ. I don't know who they belong to, sir."

"We have the orbit stabilized, Captain," said the helm.

"Communications," said Clemens. "I want to reestablish

contact with the ground." He stood up and stretched, and then suddenly realized he had been in a battle. Not much of one, but a battle just the same. Unfortunately it had all the realism of a computer game. Enemy moves revealed by the computer and his responses plugged into the computer. Nothing more real than a kid's game on old Earth. Except a mistake did not end in a demand by the machine to try again.

Wiping the sweat from his face, he turned toward the weapons console. "How many missiles were fired?"

"Last count put it at forty-eight. Two were destroyed by the enemy as they came off the launch rails. And there are indications that there were four misfires below. Total attempted attack force is fifty-four."

"Really sent up a force, didn't they?"

One of the men turned. He was a young man wearing a green uniform with his lieutenant's bars pinned to the collar. He had a moustache and a beard and looked as if he had just escaped from high school.

"Captain, they didn't need to send up much of a force. They caused us to move and to break off communications with the units on the ground. Their attack, if viewed as an extension of the guerrilla warfare tactics they used on the ground, was then a success."

Clemens nodded but didn't speak. He turned and gestured at the commo panel. "I want communications reopened with those on the ground now."

"Aye, sir."

The intelligence officer said, "We have now been forced to extend out supply lines to the ground. We're, what, three hours from launch to touchdown now?"

"Closer to five," answered the navigator.

"Captain, those ships are moving in closer," said Jenkins.

"Broadcast the standard warning. Weapons, if they persist, fire a shot across their bow."

"Aye, sir."

"Intell, I want to know who they are."

Then, as quickly as the situation developed, it evaporated. The enemy ships, if they were the enemy, suddenly reversed course. They hung close to the fleet for a moment and then accelerated away, heading out of the system.

"Plot their course," said Clemens.

"Plotted, Captain."

"Launch a scout probe to shadow them."

"Aye, sir. Probe launched."

Clemens returned to his chair and dropped in it. The screen now showed the space in front of them. Dark, black space with the stars glittering around it. There was a brightness at the bottom of the screen, part of a moon around the planet.

"Christ," said Clemens, "this is not supposed to happen." He didn't realize that he was echoing the words of Torrence on the ground.

13

JEFFERSON WAITED OUTSIDE the command center, taking in the late evening breeze and wishing that he was back on the ship where there was climate control, hot food, and no real worries. Instead he was on the planet's surface surrounded by hostile aliens and a sense of impending doom. Again he wished that Sergeant Mason were there. Mason was the soldier's soldier. A man who knew the answers to the questions and knew how to operate in all sorts of hostile environments. Mason was the man who had taught Jefferson everything he knew, but Mason had died before the lessons were complete.

Timmons, the communications specialist, came out and said, "Sir, we've lost contact with the other landing force."

Jefferson turned to face him. He wiped at the sweat on his face and asked, "You concerned about it?"

"No, sir. We're getting interference and that's it. There was no transmission from them about anything."

"You contact the fleet?"

"They report the same problem. We're not too worried about it because it seems to be some kind of natural phenomenon."

Jefferson shook his head. "I don't like it. It's too big of a coincidence. You keep trying to make contact."

"Yes, sir."

As the man returned to his post, Jefferson moved across the compound. He found Jorgenson sitting in a chair outside one of the residences. As he approached, Jefferson said, "We may have a problem. I want everyone ready to move out in thirty minutes or less."

Jorgenson got to his feet. "What is it?"

"We've lost commo with Torrence. Commo thinks it might be natural, but I don't like it. Especially with what has already happened."

Jorgenson nodded and then yelled, "Sergeant Blayfield. Form the company."

From the distance came the response. "Yes, sir."

"I'll be in the command center," said Jefferson.

"Yes, sir. I'll join you there just as soon as we are ready to move."

Jefferson returned to the command center and watched as Timmons tried to raise Torrence at the other landing site. The interference filled the screens with snow. Commo signals were blocked so that the speakers emitted only a low-grade hum that was more irritating than informative.

Then suddenly Torrence's camp broke through. A message directed toward the fleet requesting shuttles for the dead and wounded. It was a short transmission with no response from the fleet. Suddenly Captain Clemens was off the air.

Jorgenson appeared then. "We're ready to move."

Jefferson nodded and said, "Torrence was attacked. They've dead and wounded but they're back on the air." He tapped Timmons on the shoulder. "You request a status report from Major Torrence."

Timmons turned back to the screen, thought for a moment, and then said, "Rover One, this is Six. Say status."

There was no immediate response and then, just as suddenly as they had reappeared, they disappeared. The screen clouded again and the commo filled with static.

"Lost them," he said.

Jefferson said, "That's it. We know that they were attacked. We'll head out to them."

"Using the floaters?"

"Can't transfer the whole company on floaters," said Jefferson.

"Not in one lift, but we can run it in relays. It'll be faster than trying to walk it."

"Get it done," said Jefferson.

The bright glow in the distance could only mean one thing. Reardon stopped and slipped to the ground. He glanced back at Rachel and then nodded. "I think we've made it."

She crept forward, put a hand on the trunk of a tree, and said, "What are we waiting for?"

Reardon shrugged. He didn't have a good answer for that. It was just that he didn't want to go rushing down into the city without studying it. Instead, he stood, concealed in the forest, looking down at the city.

But there was something wrong with it. The lights that should have been blazing had been dimmed. Not extinguished, but not as bright as they had been. The roads leading to the city were not lined with people. They were all but deserted.

The wall around the city, made of stone and eight feet high, gave it a medieval look. Normally there were banners flying from it and people walking along it, but not tonight. It was as deserted as the rest of the city.

"Is there anyone down there?" asked Rachel.

"Has to be," said Reardon. "Too many lights on."

"Maybe they're on automatic."

"Some maybe," said Reardon, "but there's too much light. Got to be people."

"Then what are we waiting for?"

Reardon couldn't answer that. He'd seen the city. There was no sign that the aliens had attacked it. No sign of damage to the wall.

"Here's how we'll do it. I'll head down first. If I make it, you can follow. If there is something wrong, you'll have the chance to get away."

"No," said Rachel. "We'll go down together."

"But . . ."

"It makes no difference. I don't want to be left alone up here."

Reardon looked at her face, hard to see in the darkness of the night. Finally he just nodded and said, "Then we'll go down together."

"Fine."

Reardon hesitated, sure that there had to be something done to prepare. Some trick he could pull just in case, but nothing came to mind. In all his recent dreams, in all his thoughts about surviving, he'd seen this as the goal. Reach the city, rush into it and get food, drink, and safety. That was all there was to it and he'd never thought beyond that. Now, with the goal in sight, his mind was numb.

But there seemed to be no real reason to stay hidden in the trees. A short walk, half a mile, maybe a little more, and Reardon would again be surrounded by living, breathing humans. Just a short walk.

And still he was reluctant. Maybe he was savoring the moment. The goal was within reach and he wanted to enjoy that moment a little longer. Anticipation was half of the fun. Anticipation of the end of the ordeal. But once he was in the city, the anticipation would be gone.

"Let's go," said Rachel anxiously.

"Sure," he said and stepped out of the forest.

Together they walked down to the road. It was a dirt track that led up to one of the gates in the stone wall. It was a rutted road, used by wheeled vehicles, some drawn by animals that resembled horses and others using ammonia-fueled engines built for space exploration.

Reardon kept his eyes on the city, searching for some clue as to what was happening behind the walls, but nothing surfaced. The city was quiet, the only sign of inhabitants was the lights burning, throwing the glow up into the night sky.

"I don't like this," he said.

Rachel ignored that. She didn't care. The trip was over and the destination was in front of them. All she wanted was to enter the city. Get out of the forest, out of the wilds, and into the one large camp of human civilization on the planet's surface where she didn't have to be afraid every minute of every day.

As they neared the city, they slowed and Reardon finally stopped. He stood there, looking up at the heavy wooden gate. There was no sign of guards on the walls. There were a couple of cameras, each of them swinging back and forth in an automatic sequence that would last as long as the power was on and the servos held up. But no signs of human life.

"Not again," said Rachel. "I can't take it again."

"It'll be all right," said Reardon. But he was afraid that it wasn't going to be all right. He was afraid that they would enter a deserted city with the bodies of the dead sprawled on the ground.

"Contact's broken again," said the man sitting at the console.

"Us or them?" asked Torrence.

"Neither. It's that low level of electromagnetic radiation again. Suppressing everything."

"Shit," said Torrence, knowing what the increased radiation meant. She whirled and ran from the command center. "Here they come again. Everyone to your posts. Here they come again."

Just as she reached the wall, the first of the aliens appeared, running across the open ground, firing from the hip. There were lasers and old-fashioned automatic rifles, the muzzles strobing and flashing. Tracers lanced out, struck the ground or the wall, and tumbled away.

This time it was more than a probing assault. There were too many of the aliens, coming at them too fast. They were firing their weapons, but there was supporting fire coming from the trees only a few hundred meters away.

Sinclair ran up to her. "They're assaulting from the north and west too. A full company coming in both those locations."

Torrence looked at her. There were orders she wanted to give, but they were all wrong. Sinclair knew the score. Knew what to do.

"Take charge on the north and hold them out. Lay down everything," said Torrence.

"We've some cluster grenades and launchers for them."

"Break them out."

"Yes, ma'am." Sinclair whirled and ran back to the north.

Torrence ran up the steps and crouched behind the wall. She could hear the slugs slamming into it, feel the vibrations of that. She crept forward, one knee on the rough planking of the parapet. To the right, four men were popping up, firing, and ducking down. Laser beams and tracers flashed over their heads.

Torrence popped up, looked, and then dropped down, her eyes closed. She tried to replay the scene in her mind. Alien beasts running over the open ground. Clumps of them, four or five in a group, heading for specific targets.

Again she jumped but this time she fired a burst from her laser. She swung the weapon like a giant sickle, chopping off a couple at the knees. Slugs slammed into the palisade near her, chipping it.

Around her was shouting. Her soldiers giving orders to others. Men with problems. People pointing out the enemy and trying to stop it as it came running at them.

Then behind her came the popping of the grenade launchers. The small missiles shot overhead and detonated in the air. The first explosion spread the bombs of the cluster unit. The next series was the grenades themselves, filing the air with red-hot shrapnel.

Firing from outside the wall slowed. Torrence risked a peek. There were bodies of enemy aliens scattered around. The attack seemed to have been broken, but the sniping continued. Rounds smashed into the logs of the palisade. There were muzzle flashes in the distance.

"In the north," yelled someone.

Torrence glanced over her shoulder and then said, "I want half you people to remain here. The rest come with me." Then, keeping her head bowed, she worked her way to the edge of the parapet. She dropped to the ground, stood, and ran toward the north wall.

The firing there was heavy and even the cluster grenades had failed to halt the attack. The aliens swarmed up, out of the ditch and through the knee-high grass. They came in a single mass ignoring the intense firing from the camp. Dozens of them fell, but those who survived found themselves again at the base of the wall where they were protected from the people in the camp.

"Fan out," ordered Torrence. "Take whatever cover you can find and don't let anything inside the wall."

She then ran to the right and crouched in the doorway of a house that had been damaged in the fighting. Part of the roof had burned away and the windows had been broken out. She lifted the back of her hand to her face and touched her sweat-slick forehead.

For a moment, she relaxed. The aliens were at the base of the wall and weren't trying to get over it. For a moment, she could relax. She tried to think, but her mind was blank. Then thoughts were coming at her so fast that she couldn't see them or feel them. It was a grey mass that she couldn't touch and couldn't examine.

And then the moment passed. There was a shout from the parapet and one woman tumbled from it. She hit the ground, rolled, and was still. Near the body there was a single explosion and part of the wall collapsed.

The aliens began to pour through, firing, and now shouting. As they came through, they tried to spread out but the soldiers were concentrating their fire. Laser beams flashed and the enemy died. They fell in piles near the opening they had blasted through the wall. But even with the numbers of them killed, more pressed forward using the bodies of their dead for protection. They returned the fire with their own lasers or the old-fashioned rifles.

More of the enemy tried to scale the wall and were fighting with the soldiers on the parapets. There were screams now. Men and women fell, some of them trying to scramble to safety as their fellows abandoned the wall.

As the parapet was cleared, Torrence swept it with her laser. Two aliens were caught by the fire and fell, one of them over the wall and disappearing outside the camp. She kept shooting, the laser chopping through the enemy. Flames flared where the beam struck the wood of the palisade.

Sinclair appeared then. She threw herself down, rolling into a shadow near Torrence. She looked up at the other officer. "Got them stopped now."

"But for how long?" asked Torrence.

"That's the question, isn't it?"

14

THE FLOATERS SAT on the ground in the middle of the compound looking like the pontoons of an old-fashioned party boat. The soldiers, holding their weapons, sat astride the pontoons. In the rear was the pilot who controlled the craft. It was a simple thing, designed to transport soldiers and equipment short distances in environments where the more cumbersome vehicles would be impossible to use. The floaters existed for one reason. They were light, maneuverable, and they worked well in almost any location.

Jefferson stood near the door of the command center and watched as the men and women poured out of their quarters, taking up positions on the floaters. There were guards on the walls and there were people in the command center still trying to reestablish contact with Torrence and the fleet. Everyone else was preparing to move.

"We're set," reported Jorgenson.

"Course set in and locked?"

"Recon is set to go now. As soon as you order it."

"Christ," snapped Jefferson. "Send it out. You don't have to wait for permission."

Jorgenson nodded and then shouted, "Steward, get moving. Now."

A small floater holding two soldiers rose, cleared the wall, and then disappeared in the distance. There was a quiet popping as it came up off the ground that changed to an almost-inaudible hum as it began level flight.

Now Jefferson turned. The majority of the floaters were manned, the soldiers waiting as the craft sat on the ground, the lifting engines humming. "You take the lead and I'll bring up trail," said Jefferson.

"Yes, sir."

One by one, the floaters lifted off, hovered, and then crossed the wall. They never got more than fifty feet above the ground and were never moving faster than twenty or thirty miles an hour. Slow enough that an accident wouldn't be fatal but fast enough to get them to the second landing area quickly. There was no time to waste.

Jefferson, sitting astride the craft, his feet on the bar at the bottom, a metal loop in front of him to hold on to, watched as the dark ground slipped away under him. Trees, bushes, rivers, and streams all flashed by. Nothing to really look at and nothing to really see. It was too dark to see any detail but light enough to see the form.

Jefferson closed his eyes briefly, letting the wind hit him in the face. The air was humid and smelled of electricity. Ozone. And he wondered if there were storms coming. Looking up into the night sky, he could see no sign of clouds, no sign that rain was coming.

Word then passed. "We're getting close. We're getting close."

In the distance was the sound of gunfire. A quiet rattling that was hard to hear. There were patterns of light in the sky above the camp. Lasers and tracers flashing up, into the night. The battle was joined.

Then, almost immediately, the floater dipped and descended, landing near the others. It touched down on the soft ground and the engine was cut. The soldiers leapt from it, fanning out, in a loose circle to prevent ambush. Jorgenson was at the southern side of the circle with the two men who had been on the scout craft.

Crouching near them, Jefferson asked. "What have you got for me?"

One of the men turned and said, "The camp is under heavy attack on three sides. There is firing from inside, so our people are still fighting."

"Rally points?"

"I think we've spotted one of them." He pointed off to a clump of trees barely visible in the darkness. "I think there are reinforcements waiting there. They have some heavy machine guns, old slug-throwing weapons, there, firing in support of their assault forces."

"Numbers?" asked Jefferson.

"No, sir. Have no idea as to the numbers. I would say they don't have more than a battalion out here. Maybe four or five hundred individuals. More and they should have been able to overrun our people in an hour or less."

At that moment another soldier dropped to the ground near them. "Communications has failed, sir."

Jefferson looked at the newcomer. "What's that mean?"

"We're inside the circle of low-level interference," he reported. "We can't communicate with our base or with the people in front of us."

"Christ," said Jorgenson.

Jefferson pointed at the two scouts. "As soon as we start our attack, you two take your floater over the wall and let Torrence know that we're coming. They shouldn't target you since the enemy hasn't used floaters."

"Thanks," said the man sarcastically.

"Best we can do." He looked at Jorgenson. "How soon can you be ready to move?"

"Four, five minutes. Just long enough to get the people moved to this point."

"All right. Here's what we'll do. One squad here to meet the rest of the company as it comes in and to hold this point. The rest of us will move toward the enemy rally point and take that out. As we do, the scouts go over the wall. Questions?"

"We take prisoners?"

"No need for that now," said Jefferson. "We either kill them or chase them from the woods. Period."

"Yes, sir."

Jefferson pulled at the sleeve of his uniform and touched the top of his watch. The tiny ruby numbers appeared. "I want to go in five minutes."

"Yes, sir." Jorgenson ran off to alert the rest of the company.

"Do we broadcast the IFF as we go over the wall?" asked the scout.

"I would. Might not do you much good, but I'll broadcast it anyway."

"Yes, sir."

Reardon stopped at the gate and examined it. A wooden gate held together by thick iron bolts and held in position by huge iron hinges. The bolts and hinges were forged from material dug out of the ground on the planet, refined close to the mine, and then molded into useful shapes. Streaks of rust had stained the wood.

"Well," asked Rachel again.

Reardon shoved on the gate and was surprised when it began to swing. The hinges squeaked as the door opened. There was no warning shout from the inside. No noise at all.

Reardon glanced back at Rachel, and then stepped through the gate. The first thing he noticed was the odor, like that of an open sewer. Buildings lined the street but all of them were dark. Near what would have been the sidewalk were open stalls so that the first impression was of a medieval marketplace. Not exactly the clean steel and glass buildings of a spacefaring race, but the constructions of those people once they were off their home planet and on another where the industrial base was still being created.

The street was dark but in the distance he could see some light. He looked at Rachel. She asked, "What in the hell is going on here?"

"I don't know. Let's head toward the light."

"Do you think they've been attacked? Has everyone here been killed?"

Reardon shook his head. "Nope." He pointed. "There is no sign of a battle." He noticed that he was whispering, as if afraid that someone might overhear.

Together they pressed on down the street, passing one intersection that was as dark as the street they were in. They walked close to the walls of the buildings, seeking the comfort of the warm stone and listening for sounds that someone was alive on the inside.

As they approached the center of the city, they noticed that the streets were blocked. Carts, boxes, stones, and rubble had been pulled out into the street. Behind the blockade were the lights and the sound of voices.

For a moment Reardon stood still. Then he stepped out, into the middle of the street, and began to walk toward the first barricade.

"You halt right there."

Reardon did as told and slowly raised his hands. He watched the shapes moving in front of the lights. Only one man came forward, but there were others behind him, guarding him.

"Who are you?" asked the man.

"Reardon. My camp was wiped out a long while ago. I've been trying to find safety."

The man used the barrel of his rifle to point to the right. "Who's that?"

"Her name is Rachel. Same situation. Different camp."

The man came closer and examined Reardon closely. He reached out and prodded him on the shoulder and then stomach and looked deeply into his eyes. As he leaned close, a light stabbed out illuminating his face.

"Well, you look human."

"You've been having a problem with that?"

"Nope. And we don't intend to. You come with me." He gestured at Rachel. "You too, sister. But don't try anything funny 'cause we'll burn you down right then."

Reardon shrugged and started toward the barricade. He waited as one of the wagons was pulled to the side and then entered. He stopped there and looked around.

It was now an armed camp. He could see two dozen men and half that many women, all with laser rifles. Some were on the street and some were in the buildings, looking out the windows. A laser defensive system had been set up to cover the streets, if it was needed. And there were lights set in the windows, shining out onto the street.

"What in the hell is going on here?" asked Reardon.

"Hell, man, you should know. The aliens turned hostile. They've been attacking our outposts."

"All of them?"

"We evacuated a few before the aliens got to them. Every man, woman, or child from Earth is now in this city."

"You expect the aliens to attack?"

"Can you think of a reason why we shouldn't believe that? They've already made a couple of raids against us."

Reardon looked at Rachel, standing there quietly. He grinned at her and then said, "We've been in the field for a long time."

"Of course," said the man. "Come with me. We'll get you some clean clothes and some food."

"Food first," said Reardon.

"And as you're eating, maybe you can answer a few questions for us."

"I'd be happy to, but I'm afraid that I don't know much. Only what happened at my own outpost."

"Maybe you can tell me why the aliens have suddenly gotten hostile."

Reardon shook his head. "I don't have the faintest idea. They just attacked us. Without warning."

"I was afraid you'd say that."

"They're still coming," yelled someone.

Torrence shook her head. She couldn't believe that the aliens would be that persistent. She fired up at those on the parapet. One of them collapsed and then rolled off, falling to the ground. Two shot back at her, their rounds smashing into the wall near her.

Sinclair shouted, "If we don't get some help soon, we're going to lose it all."

Torrence ducked back, out of the line of fire. "Any of the communications working?"

"Still out."

Torrence wiped the back of her hand over her lips. "Couriers?"

"I doubt they'd be able to clear the walls. Too many of the aliens around."

"Shit." She glanced at the fighting on the parapets and the

firing directed into the breach in the wall. More of the enemy was pouring in. "You got an escape plan?"

"If it looks as if we're going to be overrun, it's everyone on his own. Escape and evade as best you can."

"Not much of a plan."

"No, but it's all I've got."

"Okay, you cover me. I'm going to the command center to see if anything's changed." She started to get up.

Sinclair grabbed her arm. "How long do you expect us to hold out?"

Torrence sank back and looked into the other officer's eyes. "I expect you to hold on as long as possible. We give the order to abandon the camp and a lot of our people are going to die. More than if we can hold on here."

"No reason to hold on here," said Sinclair.

"Except that Jefferson knows where we are and that if we try to get out we're going to be cut down individually. This way it costs the enemy something."

"Stupid damn reason for hanging on," she said.

"Better than nothing." Torrence started to get up again and then said, "Once I find out what's happening at the command center, we'll know more. Any red light, flare, whatever, and it means that we've got to get out of here."

"Understood," said Sinclair. She hesitated and then added, "Good luck."

Torrence listened to the firing and watched the tracers and laser beams around her. When it looked as if there was a break, a hold in the firing, she took off running, ducking low. She dodged right and then left and finally dived in the door. She rolled once and came up on a knee.

The commo specialist was sitting on the floor, his back to the console. His rifle was clutched in his hands and he was staring at the door, but making no attempt to fire out of it. He stared at her.

"You get through to anyone?"

"Comm is out," he said dully.

"You tried lately?" She stood up and moved to the right, out of line with the door.

"No good. Comm is out."

"Have you tried lately?"

"No. Can't get through. Equipment is wrecked and no way to repair it."

There was a sudden burst of firing. Slugs flashed through the door and slammed into the plastic walls with quiet thuds. The man rolled right, flattening himself.

Torrence ignored that. She leapt over the broken chair and ruined equipment on the floor. She punched two of the buttons and flipped a switch. There was current to the equipment, but no response to her actions.

Whirling, she yelled, "You've got to help me."

"No good. No good at all."

Torrence wanted to shoot the man. Lying on the floor, protecting his head with his hands, would do no good. Not with the enemy storming the walls. They had to do something, and if they couldn't make contact with the fleet or with Jefferson, then they were on their own. They had to find their own solutions or they were all going to die.

Again she tried to work the equipment but the screens, the ones that hadn't been ruined by the enemy or in the fighting, remained blank. Nothing on them. No way to clear them. No signals coming in.

"Get up," yelled Torrence. "Hurry."

A round slammed into the console no more than six inches from her hand. Bits of metal, circuit boards, and plastic exploded out from it. One of them clipped Torrence but she ignored the sudden flash of pain.

Now she did turn and kick at the man. "You lie there and we're all going to die. You get up and maybe we can get some help."

The man rolled over and looked up at her. His face was pale, the color having drained from it. There were black rings around his eyes, making it look as if he had already died.

"Come on, chicken," she sneered. "Get up and help or lay there and die."

The man didn't move right away. Then slowly, he climbed to his feet and took his place at the console. He leaned over it, touched it, and then began to work.

"I'll cover you," said Torrence. She moved to the door and crouched there, watching as the aliens poured over the wall and ran along the parapets. Firing was slowing as more of the soldiers were killed or wounded. The aliens were firing into some of the buildings. Fires were burning now and in the flickering half-light the shadows seemed to dance and sway.

"You'd better make it fast," said Torrence. "We don't have a lot of time."

The man glanced over his shoulder at her. "I'm doing the best I can."

"Let's hope it's enough," Torrence said.

15

WITH JEFFERSON LEADING, the men and women of the company slipped through the forest carefully, listening to the sounds of the battle coming from the camp to the north. They moved slowly, trying to avoid making noise. The point was out, forty meters in front of them, marking the path.

Twenty minutes after they started, they stopped at the top of a ridge line that overlooked the valley where the camp had been built. Jefferson crawled to the top and looked down. The forest stopped short of the walls. There was a copse of trees that could be a rally point and there was a tree line where the machine guns fired in support of the assault troops. Tracers and lasers flashed from the trees, the rounds and the beams slamming into the wooden stockade.

"Over there," whispered the scout. "Fifty to a hundred individuals."

Jefferson twisted around and used his starlight binoculars. There were trees, bushes, but only a few individuals moving. "You sure?"

"Most of them are lying chilly. Not moving, but they're there. No doubt about it."

"Can we get down there?"

The scout shrugged. "Cover looks good but you try to move

thirty people through the bush and there is going to be some noise. Might be covered by the battle. Might not."

Firing from the camp seemed to increase. More of the aliens were attacking it. Some seemed to have gained access to it. Time was becoming important.

"Get ready to move," said Jefferson. He slipped to the rear and then stood, hurrying to the main body of the company. He hesitated and then located the commo specialist.

"You have contact with the people on the inside?"

The man shook his head. "Nothing. Absolutely nothing."

Jefferson found Jorgenson crouched down, facing to the rear. He held his rifle in both hands, the but on the ground as if it was supporting him. "Let's get ready to move."

Jorgenson looked up and then stood. "Force is getting whittled down."

"Can't be helped. We've got to move."

Jorgenson nodded and moved off, alerting the NCOs. Finished, he returned. As he did, Jefferson started back up the hill, toward the scouts there.

The attacking force worked its way up the hill and then stopped, fanning out again. Jefferson leaned close to Jorgenson and said, "Once we begin the attack, once the firing erupts, I want the scout flyer heading into the camp. I don't want Torrence to open up on us."

"Consider it done."

Jefferson nodded and then moved to the right, to where the scout waited. "Let's do it."

"Yes, sir."

Now the whole force was on its feet, moving to the crest of the ridge line. Using the forest there for cover, they crossed it and began to move down into the valley. They veered to the right, avoiding a stone cliff twenty to thirty meters high. They slipped around it, using a place where it had collapsed, providing them with a slope that was covered with thick, tall grass and several flowering bushes.

When they reached the valley floor, still undetected, they moved to the left, staying close to the hill and working their way toward the enemy rally point. They reached the edge of the forest where the aliens hid and fanned out behind it. Then, as one, they moved in, creeping closer to the enemy soldiers.

Jefferson soon lost sight of everyone around him with the exception of the men or women just to his right and left. Three people and that was it. Now it seemed that the company had been cut down to those few people.

Then, in front of him, he saw one of the alien soldiers. It stood, its back to him, watching as its fellows tried to take the camp from Torrence and the others. Jefferson slipped closer until he was sure of the shot. Then, aiming at the center of the alien's back, he fired his laser once. It was a short burst and an effective one. The creature spasmed as the beam burned into it. It stood up, its muscles suddenly rigid in shock and pain. Then it fell forward with a quiet thud.

Around it, its fellows turned to look. They didn't understand what was happening. Jefferson saw another as it moved, stepping toward the dead creature. Again he fired a quick burst and the creature tumbled back, into a bush with dried leaves that rattled as the alien dropped on it.

Around him the firing came suddenly. Ruby beams no wider than pencils flashing through the trees. Aliens fell. It was a strange, quiet battle, defined only by the flashing of the lasers and the rattles of death as the enemy died.

Jefferson slipped deeper into the forest, searching for more of the enemy. He saw one of them standing at the opposite edge of the trees, its hands up to its eyes as if it had a pair of binoculars with which to watch the battle. Jefferson slipped to one knee, raised his weapon, and aimed, firing quickly. The beam struck the creature in the center of the back. The cloth it wore, or maybe its own flesh, flared under the heat of the beam. It pitched forward, out of the trees and into the open as it died. The flames on its back died quickly.

Jefferson kept pushing forward, glancing right and left to make sure that the men or women were there with him. He reached the edge of the forest and stopped, crouching in the shadows near a tall tree.

From the right, over the top of the ridge where they had been waiting, the two-man scout floater flashed. It dropped down, following the contours of the land, staying just above the tops of the trees. It was aimed directly at the walls of the camp. Jefferson hoped that the defenders would be smart enough not to open fire.

Jorgenson appeared then. "We've secured this forest. Aliens are all dead."

"Then have the soldiers begin to target the aliens in the fields around us. Take out as many as you can."

"Yes, sir."

Torrence watched as four of the aliens fell from the parapet. Two more ran along it, toward the steps. One of them threw himself down, rolling over, but the other leapt to the stairs. She turned and looked back into the command center.

"You got anything?"

"No. Commo is out. Completely out." He kicked the base of the console and part of the plastic pedestal shattered.

From outside, someone shouted, "Something's coming!"

Torrence whirled and ran out. She saw the scout floater appear over the wall. As it did, she shouted, "Don't fire! Don't fire!"

The craft tilted, dived, and then hit the ground near the command center. Firing from the parapet erupted, the slugs churning the ground near the floater. The two passengers leapt off and scrambled for cover.

Torrence turned her weapon on the parapet, firing in short bursts. "Cover them!" she yelled. "Cover them."

More firing came from the ground. Lasers against the old-fashioned weapons. Tracers and beams of light crisscrossing. And then it began to taper slightly.

As it did, Torrence was out the door, running across the open ground. She dived for cover as two aliens fired at her, the bullets tearing at the heel of her boot and smashing into the ground behind her. She rolled once and came up face-to-face with one of the scouts.

"What the hell are you idiots doing?" she demanded.

"Orders from the colonel," said the man, grinning. "Came to save your butt from the alien attackers."

"Then where in the hell is he?"

"Outside the wall. Didn't want some trigger-happy soldier to cut him down."

"The colonel's here?"

The man hitchhiked a thumb over his shoulder. "Outside the

wall, at one of the alien rally points. No commo with you inside here."

"Commo is all out."

"Right. Anyway, he's going to be coming in soon and didn't want to get shot to pieces doing it."

"Why land out there?" asked Torrence.

"Hell, Major, you'll have to ask him that yourself though I suspect it was to surprise the aliens by hitting them in the rear and to give us a chance to warn you about us coming in."

Torrence stuck her head up and looked around. There was still shooting, but it had slackened. Maybe that was a response by the aliens to the attack in their rear. Or maybe it was just wishful thinking on her part.

"I'll alert the others," she said.

The man nodded and said, "We'll wait right here."

Torrence shot them a glance and then had to laugh. She didn't say anything else to them. Instead she leapt to her feet and ran back toward the command center. This time there was no one shooting at her. She dived inside and yelled, "Help's on the way. Watch for our people in the field." And then she was up again and out the door.

Jefferson watched the floater fly over the wall and disappear into the camp. As soon as it was gone, he turned to Jorgenson. "Let's get this taken care of."

Jorgenson moved to the right and ordered, "Let's take out the machine guns. Everyone up. Let's go."

They turned their direction of attack, slipping from the clump of the forest to the line that stretched out, paralleling the wall of the camp. Jorgenson led the assault, laser rifle firing as he ran toward the enemy machine gunners. The roar bubbled in his throat and escaped his lips. He screamed his anger at the enemy, firing at them as he ran straight for them.

The machine guns that had been directed at the camp spun. Tracers flashed out. Those that were wide looked like golf balls. Those that were closer were bigger than basketballs. Jorgenson ducked and dodged, screaming as he fired from the hip.

He ran into the tree line, leapt over a fallen log like a hurdler going for the gold. He stumbled once and found himself among the enemy. He fired, the laser stabbing out. Flames flared where the beam touched the ground or the trees or the bodies of the aliens. One of them came at him, swinging a club, and Jorgenson burned him down. He killed another and then another.

All around him his soldiers were engaged in the fighting. Men and women shooting at the shapes in the darkened forest. Soldiers attacking the machine gunners and their assistants. Beams flashed and machine guns fired. Tracers bounced high, tumbling upward into the night.

Jorgenson swung on an alien and fired but the beam was wide, missing the creature. It leapt forward and bowled him over. Jorgenson lost the grip on his weapon. It fell to the ground, disappearing. Jorgenson thrust with his hips and tried to roll, but the creature held him. Now Jorgenson tried to free his pistol, but it was trapped between the ground and his body. He tried for his knife. The blade came free and he plunged it into the chest of the alien.

But the creature didn't seem to notice the wound. It lifted its hand over its head and brought it down, striking Jorgenson. Pain flared in his chest and suddenly he couldn't get a breath. He tried to kick the creature free, but it settled down. It began hammering at his face and his shoulders with its clublike fists. Pain exploded in his body and there were flashes of bright light in his eyes. For a moment longer he tried to defend himself but then the colors faded and blackness began to descend.

Jefferson followed the attack into the tree line. He ran toward the rear of it and then stopped. Shadows were moving all around him. Some of them seemed human and some seemed alien but most of them were impossible to identify. Jefferson was afraid to fire fearing he would hit his own people as they mixed in with the enemy.

He watched as two creatures seemed to unite, the darkness hiding their shapes. One of them stumbled away and the other stood straight. It turned, facing Jefferson, and he knew that it wasn't human. He fired from the hip, the beam punching through the alien. It grabbed his stomach, moaned low in its throat, and then fell.

He moved then, finding two aliens lying behind a machine

gun but neither of them shooting. The assistant held the linked ammo up off the ground as the gunner slowly swung the barrel searching for a target.

Jefferson didn't hesitate. He slipped to one knee and aimed at the back of the enemy gunner. He pulled the trigger and the beam touched the alien. As it did, he swung it toward the assistant who was just beginning to react. The laser slashed his side like an old-fashioned broadsword. The creature started to stand, screaming, but then collapsed to a whimpering heap as its blood drained from it.

Before Jefferson could move, the firing around him seemed to stop. No more hammering of machine guns and no flashing of lasers. The enemy had been overrun and eliminated.

Moving forward, he found one of the NCOs. "Where's Captain Jorgenson?"

"Dead."

"Shit." Jefferson touched the man. "It's up to us then. Get the people ready to move out."

"Where are we going?"

"Into the camp now. Floaters in. We can head in and help out there."

"Yes, sir."

The soldiers reassembled at the edge of the tree line. Their ranks had been thinned by the attack, but there were still enough of them left to do the job. Jefferson waited until they were ready, and then with a single motion of his hand signaled them out into the open.

Then they began to run. The first few steps were slow, but as they got out into the open, they began to run faster. They leapt over the obstacles, heading for the protection of the walls and the camp.

There were some aliens around, but most of those involved in the attack were now inside the camp trying to eliminate the humans there. Jefferson ran with the others, leaping the bodies of the enemy aliens slain in the rush to the walls. He dodged the sporadic firing. He ran to the left, toward one of the gates in the wall. And then he found himself crouching there, waiting for the others to gather around him.

He hesitated at the gate for a moment. And then, with the soldiers who had made it, Jefferson shoved his way through the gate. As he reached the interior of the camp, he saw the aliens on the parapets and near the hole blown in the wall. Firing came from the doors and the windows of the houses and the buildings. Humans were lying behind whatever cover they could find, shooting up at the enemy. The air was thick with the smell of burnt flesh and cordite. The automatic weapons of the enemy were hammering, just as they had been, the rounds churning the ground around the humans.

"Let's take them," yelled Jefferson. He leapt forward, screaming, firing from his hip. He ran toward the middle of the camp where the command center was located.

As he did, the rest of the company fanned out, firing up at the enemy. The increase was enough to turn the tide. Those aliens not cut down in the first few minutes scrambled to escape. They jumped over the walls and ran for the gates, trying to get out. The attack disintegrated within moments of Jefferson and his company reaching the camp.

Jefferson dodged right and left and leapt forward, rolling into the room. He sat up and looked at the commo operator. "Where's Major Torrence?"

"Don't know, sir. She ran out of here a little while ago."

Jefferson stood up and brushed the dirt from his uniform. "You able to break through?"

"No, sir. Commo is dead as hell."

"Keep at it."

"Yes, sir."

Jefferson moved to the door and looked out. The sun was beginning to come up. There was a brightness in the sky that hadn't been there earlier. The dead were black shapes lying on a graying ground. Smoke drifted from a dozen small fires. But the firing had died away. The enemy had abandoned the camp.

Jefferson stepped out and then stopped. Two shapes were coming at him and behind them a third. He recognized Torrence as she got nearer.

"It was pretty hairy for a while there," she said as she got close.

"You okay?"

"Fine. We've taken some heavy casualties," she said.

Jefferson nodded and then thought of some of the conversations they'd had. He thought about the offer she'd made earlier, when telling him to forget about Norris. He thought about some of the things they'd said to each other, but now, with everyone standing around listening, he could say nothing about that.

"Where's Sinclair?"

"With the medic, seeing how many of the badly wounded are going to have to be evacked." She stopped and then added, "We didn't think you'd know what was happening here. With the commo out, we thought we were on our own."

"Right now, we all are. We'll have to do something to get a message up to Clemens."

Suddenly Torrence laughed. "Glad you could make it."

Seeing that the battle was over, for the moment, Jefferson nodded. "Glad that we could help."

16

CLEMENS WATCHED THE unidentified ships fall away in the view screen and wondered why he was running. There was no indication that the ships were hostile, and at the range they were at now, they were no immediate threat. Evasive actions and defensive maneuvers could be initiated long before they could hit him with anything deadly.

"Get the regimental intelligence officer up here," he said. "Now."

"Aye, sir," said Jenkins. She touched the internal commo, and spoke into it softly.

While he was waiting, Clemens turned to his second officer, Tabor. "You have a reading on those ships yet?"

"They might be warships in a lightweight destroyer class. There is nothing like them in any of our fleets. Weapons? Some beamed, probably without much punch, and nuclear-tipped missiles. Our shields will be adequate for their beams and our targeting computers should be able to engage and destroy any missiles launched at us."

"Thank you."

The hatch to the bridge opened and Captain Carter entered. He stood there for a moment. Clemens looked at him and then waved him forward. "You're intelligence?"

"Yes, sir."

"Jenkins, give me a view of the missle complexes on the ground." When the view came up, Clemens asked, "What can you tell me about those?"

Carter stared and then moved closer. He turned and asked, "Can I get a closer look?"

"Jenkins."

"Magnification ten." The view changed showing the gross outlines of the complexes on the ground.

"Magnification fifty."

Now Carter could see the missiles on their launch rails. The view was good enough to show him the fins on the missiles and the insignia painted on them. He crouched there and studied the screen carefully.

Finally he stood. "Not much to tell. You have what appears to be a fairly standard surface-to-air missile that has the capability of space intercepts. Look to be modeled after the Euro BL-27. I would be surprised if their range capabilities were much more than a hundred, hundred and fifty miles. Certainly nuclear-tipped but I see nothing to suggest anything more sophisticated."

"Could a landing force take out the complex?"

"Hell, Captain, a single, well-placed bomb could do that. Hit the targeting radar or complex and the whole site will be blinded."

"Can you identify the command center from here?"

Carter turned his attention back to the missile site and then shook his head. "The problem is that I have to base everything I tell you on my own experience. Since this is an alien site, my guess might be wrong unless it happens to be the BL-27."

"Then you advocate a landing force to take out the site."

Carter laughed and shook his head. Then, holding his hands up as if he was surrendering, said, "I advocate nothing. I merely advise, based on my knowledge of various systems and capabilities."

"I like the way you bounce the ball back into my court," said Clemens. "I'll want a landing party designated to take out three missile sites. The three that fired on us."

"Excuse me, sir," said Carter, "but that is outside my authority. I request missions to suppress possible hazards, but

I do not have the authority to approve the missions. My advice here would be to use small nuclear weapons so that the electromagnetic pulse will take out the electronics."

"You tell me what you want," said Clemens, "and I'll approve it."

"What about Colonel Jefferson?"

"He's on the ground and unavailable to approve anything," said Clemens. "You get this organized and give me the information."

Carter turned to look at the screen again and then stroked his chin as he thought. "My advice is to use the nuclear approach. It's safer than landing on the ground."

"I'll want it in writing," said Clemens. "Jenkins, accompany Carter and help him arrange this."

"Aye, sir." She stood up.

"You just write up your recommendations along with all supporting documentation and bring it up to me."

"Yes, sir."

As the two of them left the bridge, Clemens said, "Now, why don't we see if we can get rid of those enemy ships."

"Aye, sir," said the weapons officer.

Reardon, now wearing a clean jumpsuit, having had the chance to shower, sat at a table spread with food. Lots of food, most of it grown locally, but some of it imported from Earth and the surrounding planets. Rachel was with him, but she had slumped against the high back of the chair and fallen asleep. The sudden release of the strain of hiding from the enemy had relaxed her to the point that she could no longer stay awake no matter how much food was on the table in front of her.

"What did you see?" asked Jackson, one of the armed men sitting with him.

There were four others, sitting around the table, all drinking coffee. The room was fairly small, just large enough for the table in the center of it, the chairs around it, and a path so that everyone could get out easily.

Jackson was a big man, his face nearly hidden in a growth of black beard. Even with the colony in the summer months, Jackson had his beard. It was easier to keep it than to shave it off when the weather turned warm.

"See?" said Reardon, eating a sandwich.

"Around you. After your camp was overrun. What did you see?"

"I saw the aliens hunting down our people and killing them." He noticed the look of horror that passed among the men. "No torture. Quick kills," he added quickly.

"But they were dead, just the same," said Goswell. He was a smaller man with thinning blond hair, bushy black eyebrows, and thin, sharp features. His hands were constantly in motion as if he were afraid to let them rest.

"Dead just the same," repeated Reardon, "but it was quick."

Jackson asked, "Were there many armed creatures out there?"

"I saw some and avoided them. I saw no large forces if that's what you're driving at, but then I was trying to avoid contact with the aliens." He took a drink of the water and set the cup down. "Hell, I'd just seen a large force, maybe two, three hundred, attack my camp. I wanted to stay away from that."

"Then you don't know if they were coming here."

Reardon leaned back in the chair and closed his eyes momentarily. When he opened them again, he said, "I would think that you can assume they're coming here. They hit Rachel's camp and killed everyone. You said they'd hit some of the others. They're coming here."

"But we're stronger," said Jackson. "We've more people and better arms."

Reardon laughed. "You think that matters. They won't attack here until they're sure they can take the place. Numbers won't mean anything if we don't get military help."

"It's on the way," said Jackson. "I have been assured that a fleet has been dispatched."

"They'd better hurry," said Reardon.

"You know something?" asked Goswell.

"No," said Reardon tiredly. "No, I don't know anything."

Jackson took over again. "Do you know why the aliens would turn suddenly hostile?"

Reardon finished his sandwich. He patted his lips with a napkin and then shook his head. "I haven't the foggiest notion. All I know is that they hit our camp, the defensive system did nothing to stop them, and then they killed everyone inside the walls that they could find."

"Okay," said Jackson. He pointed at Bavley and Kemp who had said nothing during the interview. "I want you to begin gathering everyone into the inner circle. No excuses. No stragglers. Everyone inside the circle where we can protect them."

"Okay," said Bavley.

"And I want this completed in the next three hours. Kemp, I want you to get to the commo center and try to raise that Earth fleet. I want to know their ETA and how many soldiers they've brought with them. Remind them that we have children here."

Reardon broke in. "Do you think that's going to make a difference?"

"It had better," said Jackson, "because I'm not sure how much protection we can give our people."

"I hope you can do better than I did."

"We're going to try."

"Turn the fleet," said Clemens. "I want *Hornet* and *Enterprise* forward with *Intrepid* held back to protect the troop ships."

"Aye, sir."

"Helm, plot an intercept course on those unidentified ships."

"Aye, sir." There was a hesitation and then, "Course plotted and laid in."

"Commo, issue the orders to *Hornet* and *Enterprise*."

"Captains Rollins and Pearlmen have confirmed the orders, sir."

"Helm, initiate intercept, now."

"Aye."

"Jenkins . . ." Clemens looked toward Jenkins's station and then remembered he'd sent her off with Carter. He snapped his fingers at the young man who had taken over for Jenkins.

"Hauptmann, Captain."

"Give me visual on this."

"Aye, sir."

The view on the screen changed, now showing him space outside the ship. In the distance, little more than points of light that moved faster than the starfield behind them, were the unidentified ships. As the fleet picked up speed, the points of light began to take on shape and size. They made no move to escape.

"Give me a clear frequency," said Clemens.

"Frequency opened, sir."

Clemens nodded, and thought for a moment. Then he said, "Ships off our bow, please identify yourselves. Close transmission."

"Not the friendliest of messages, Captain," said Hauptmann.

"Friendliness is irrelevant in this situation." He nodded and the frequency was opened again. "Please identify yourself or I'll be forced to fire on you. Close transmission."

Clemens waited but there was no response. He turned and said, "Weapons, put a blast across their bows. No closer than one thousand kilometers. Thermonuclear."

"Aye, sir . . . Ready."

"Fire."

"Fired."

Clemens watched the nuclear-tipped missile flash into view, accelerating toward the unidentified ships. As it approached them, it suddenly vanished in a burst of bright light. It turned into a glowing ball of fire that spread in all directions and slowly faded.

"Anything on any frequency?" asked Clemens.

"I'm monitoring nothing. No transmissions from those ships, though I'm picking up increased transmissions on the ground."

"What about the missile sites there?"

"No, sir. Doesn't seem to be affecting them."

"Captain, the unidentified ships are turning toward us."

Clemens watched the ships begin to turn. It wasn't a sudden reversal of course or a tight turn, but a looping maneuver that brought them around to face the fleet. Clemens was aware of the old adage that said anything pointed at him was hostile, but the ships had done nothing except appear in space near him. They had not fired at him, but then they had not answered his message. It could be that they didn't understand it.

"Shields going up," said Hauptmann.

"Launch detection."

Clemens watched as two points of light blasted away from the lead ship. Two pinpricks of light headed straight at him. "Targeting?"

"On it, Captain."

"Destroy them."

"Aye, sir."

A moment later both the points of light blazed brightly and briefly. The balls of fire were nowhere near as spectacular as the one caused by Clemens's warning shot.

"Launch detection," said a voice.

This time it seemed that the side of one of the ships had burst into flame. A series of pinpoints came racing at them. A dozen of them, spreading out slightly.

"Targeting."

"I have them, Captain. Prepared to fire."

"You have permission."

One by one the oncoming missiles were targeted and destroyed. They flared briefly, flashed, and then were gone. When the last of them had vanished from the screen, the targeting officer said calmly, "Threat eliminated."

"Targeting, let's take them out now."

"Aye, sir."

"Captain," said Hauptmann, his voice unnaturally high. "I have multiple targets coming from behind the ships."

"Sir, we have launch detection from the ground. Ten, twelve, fifteen coming up at us."

Then, on the screen, the unidentified ships fired another salvo. Missiles leapt at him. They described thin arcs in space as their engines burned.

"Targeting?"

"Working, sir. Which targets have priority?"

"Closest first, Lieutenant. Always the closest first."

Suddenly the first of the new targets seemed to split apart and the fragments began corkscrewing, their engines tiny, almost invisible points of light bobbing and weaving in space.

"Take them out," said Clemens. "Now."

One of the missiles detonated and as it did the others began to corkscrew. Instead of taking them out with ease, the beam weapons were missing. The missiles were getting closer.

"Targeting," said Clemens, getting nervous for the first time.

Two missiles flashed from the ship flying straight for the incoming weapons. One of them detonated, the radiation expanding outward, seeming to absorb everything it touched. As it engulfed two enemy missiles, both detonated, adding to the brightness and to the shock wave.

"Reverse engines," said Clemens.

"Aye, sir."

Another of the enemy missiles detonated, hit by a beam. As it exploded, another veered into it and, caught in the radiation, disintegrated.

"Missiles," said Clemens.

"Aye, sir."

"Target the lead ship. I want a spread of four missiles set to hit him in the bow, side, and stern."

"Aye, sir."

"Ground missiles now in range, Captain."

"Lasers, independently target and destroy those missiles. Targeting?"

The situation on the main screen hadn't changed. The missiles launched by the unidentified ships were still rushing forward, on a collision course with him.

Before targeting replied, another three missiles disappeared in bursts of bright light. Two additional weapons flew into the expanding debris clouds and vanished.

"We're working."

The missiles were getting closer than they had during the first attack. They had grown from points of light to small, glowing objects.

Hornet appeared at the bottom of the screen. There were flashes along the side of it and the incoming missiles began to explode. One by one they vanished until the threat had been eliminated.

And as that happened, the first of the missiles launched by Clemens erupted into bright light. The wave reached out and touched the enemy ship. It seemed to lift the nose. The craft shook itself and broke free of the radiation just as it was hit again.

Now the bow came up but the body seemed to stay straight.

Flames rushed along one side of it, spreading rapidly. Pale blue flames burned off the trapped oxygen. The ship shuddered, seemed to collapse in on itself, and then blew up in a flash of light that filled the screen, blanking everything.

Clemens raised a hand, shielding his eyes. He turned his head to the side, and as the white light began to fade, Clemens turned back. The missiles that had been coming at him were gone, some of them destroyed in the explosion of the ship and the rest eliminated by the targeting.

When the screen cleared, one of the enemy ships was gone. There was a black cloud of debris slowly expanding. The remaining ships had turned and were fleeing.

"Spread of missiles, proximity fuses," said Clemens.

"Ready, Captain."

"Fire them."

"Missiles away," said one of the officers.

Hornet fired on the fleeing ships and the upcoming missiles. One by one, they detonated, flashing like the best of the Fourth of July displays.

Clemens watched the last of the missiles vanish and fell back in his chair. Sweat soaked his uniform and beaded on his forehead. His stomach was tied in knots, but there didn't seem to be anything else coming up at them.

"Screen is blank," said Hauptmann.

"Targeting?"

"Nothing, Captain. Screens are empty."

"Helm, reverse and plot course back to the troop ships."

"Aye, sir."

Clemens rubbed a hand over his face. "Get intell up here."

"Ship or infantry?"

"Ship. I want the tapes replayed for her and her analysis of it within an hour."

The commo officer turned and said, "I've gotten through to the ground."

Clemens nodded and said, "Finally. Put them through." He turned to face the screen and waited.

17

"I HAVE CONTACT with the fleet, Colonel."

Jefferson leapt into the command center and rushed the desk. On the screen he saw Clemens. Just a head and shoulders view.

"Captain, we've been trying to establish contact with you for the last fifteen minutes."

"Sorry, Colonel, but we've been having trouble. Attacks from both spaceborne launch platforms and from the ground."

"Captain, we need shuttles down here now. We've wounded and dead and I want to confer with you."

"Certainly, Colonel." Clemens leaned so that he was no longer visible on the screen. There was a hurried discussion, almost audible. Clemens reappeared and said, "I'll have a shuttle down there inside of an hour."

"Sooner would be better," said Jefferson. "Some of the badly wounded need treatment in the medical facilities on board the ship."

"I'll do what I can."

Jefferson nodded and said, "Any damage to the fleet?"

"Negative. They didn't get close. We're still ready to fight, and all weapons are fully charged."

"Keep me informed."

"Certainly."

Jefferson turned then and walked out into the compound. The soldiers were moving around, checking the bodies, picking up the weapons, making sure that the aliens still on the inside were dead.

Torrence stood, a hand on the corner of a wall, leaning there. Her rifle was held in her other hand. She looked tired. Her uniform was torn and dirty.

"Shuttles are arranged. I want you to accompany me up to the fleet for an intell briefing with Carter."

"There's a lot of work to be done here."

"Granted, but Sinclair can handle it. She's a competent officer."

"What are you going to do about Jorgenson?"

"We'll move his exec up, unless you've got someone else in mind. For the moment, Sinclair will have tactical command of both companies in a sort of operational battalion. We'll make the changes later."

Torrence nodded. "Then we're going to consolidate the two forces."

"Both of them here until we come up with a battle plan."

Torrence took a deep breath. "I got to tell you. I thought we'd bought the whole thing this time. When the commo went out, it seemed that we were through."

"They've got a good jamming system. Wipes us out completely," said Jefferson. "Makes you wonder where they got it all of a sudden." He glanced around and then added, "We've got to secure one of the fields for the shuttle. I'll get with the commo and get the rest of Jorgenson's company moved here."

Torrence sat down, her head between her knees. She looked up at Jefferson, her face bathed in sweat. "It's worse than I remember. Much worse."

"It always is."

Torrence took a deep breath. She looked as if she was going to say something, but then didn't. She just stared off into the growing light. Finally she said, "I don't think I can stand this butcher's yard too many more times."

Reardon stood at the door and watched the activity in the street. He'd seen the same thing once before and that had been on Earth. A rumor had swept the city that the food stores had run

out and that the army was going to keep everyone inside
the city limits whether they starved or not. No one waited for
the rumor to be confirmed or denied. They had spread into the
streets prepared to fight their way clear. The activity in front of
him had the same frenzied, ill-defined goals. No one knew
what to do but everyone agreed he had to do something and he
had to do it right now.

Everyone was awake and in the street. They were stacking
equipment, supplies, everything they could move, out of the
structures and building more barricades. There were parties
tearing down the outskirts of the city. Ripping it apart,
flattening it, and setting it on fire to create open fields for the
enemy to cross. Making the city into a fortress.

Rachel came up behind him, her eyes still half closed and
her voice fuzzed with sleep. "What's going on?"

"Panic," said Reardon. "Pure panic. They have no idea
what they're doing, but they're all out there doing something."

She moved into the doorway, blinked at the sun, and then
wrapped her arms around herself. "We're not safe yet, are
we?"

"We're better off than we were, but no one's going to be safe
until the army gets here." He looked down at her. "If they
don't make it, we're going to be in serious trouble."

Then, almost as if to prove him wrong, there was a shout
outside. A single shout that became two, and then three,
spreading outward until it infected everyone outside. They all
stood in the streets, men, women, and children, screaming and
clapping and laughing.

A man ran past and Reardon stepped out. "Hey! What's
going on?"

"Army's in orbit. Army's arrived. Commo just confirmed it.
We're all saved." The man then ran off, screaming at the top
of his voice, heading for a group of people standing in the
street.

"You think it's true?" asked Rachel.

"Don't know," said Reardon. "Army had to show up
sometime, especially since we all sent off distress signals.
Hell, I would have expected them all here before now."

Those who had been working outside the barricades were

slowly caught up in the celebration. They stopped working and poured back over the makeshift obstructions.

"I don't like the looks of this, Rachel. Anytime people begin to rely on others, outsiders, they're in trouble."

"So what should we do?"

Reardon drained the juice in the glass he held. "The smart thing would be to get out of the city. Get clear before the aliens attack."

"But we're not going to do that?"

"We're going to stay right where we are," said Reardon. "I don't want to survive in the forest for another three or four weeks."

"Then we'll join the celebration?"

"Let's not be stupid, either."

Jefferson stood just under the wall, outside the camp, watching as the shuttle approached. It came in shallow, avoiding the trees where the enemy had hid, flying a crooked path over the open areas, shooting for a touchdown two hundred meters from the trees and a hundred meters from the wall. The two engines roared and filled the sky with a thick, black smoke. Operating close to the ground in the heavy atmosphere reduced the efficiency of engines designed to work best at high altitudes in rarefied atmosphere.

As soon as the shuttle had rolled to a stop, the rear ramp was down and people were running toward it. Some of them carried stretchers with the more seriously injured on them. Others were the walking wounded, taking themselves to the ship. Jefferson touched Torrence on the arm and said, "Come on, Vicky, time to go."

Together they walked across the ash field that had been a grassy plain before the fighting had started. Their feet kicked up tiny puffs of dust and black ash, coating their boots and the pants to the knees with a black residue. Walking up the ramp, they left black footprints that mixed with those of the others.

In the back of the shuttle, the soldiers sat on the floor, waiting to get off the planet. A couple of medics hovered around the more seriously injured. As Jefferson entered, he noticed that his regiment had the look of a defeated force, their heads were down. There was no talking among them.

He stopped at the top of the ramp and said, "Hey! You're the lucky ones. Back to the fleet. Good food and air-conditioning."

"We lost, Colonel," said one of them.

"Lost hell. We won. We hold the field. We hold the camp. And alien casualties are twice as high as ours. It was the aliens who fled, licking their wounds."

"Yeah," yelled a man, getting to his feet. "Colonel's right about that. We done good."

"Damn right," said Jefferson. "You done very good. Held out against a superior force and drove them away. Nothing to be ashamed of."

"Right, Colonel," said someone else.

The loadmaster chime din. "Sir, if you'll sit down, we'll get out of here."

Jefferson found a place on the floor and sat. It was a soft floor, with soft walls, designed to absorb the forces of the takeoff without breaking the bones of the passengers.

Torrence sat down next to him, leaned back, and closed her eyes. "Wake me when we get there."

"Of course."

There was a warning bell and the shuttle began to move. First it was just a slow roll that sped up as they moved the plain. They lifted from the ground, flew along in the ground effect as they picked up more speed. Then, suddenly, the nose tilted up and the booster engines kicked in. For a moment they seemed to hang suspended there and then began a rapid climb out. Jefferson felt himself pushed back, down, into the soft padding of the floor.

But this wasn't like the deployment drops where he was wrapped in a coffin-sized pod. This was wide open, almost like a passenger jet on old Earth. It was a little more uncomfortable because no one worried about inconveniencing soldiers, but it was better than the pods. Much better. He could look into the calm faces of those around him and take some comfort in that. Being with people, able to see people, was much better than being alone in a pod.

The rumbling of the engines lessened and the trajectory slackened as they reached the upper atmosphere. Jefferson began to relax. He stretched out flat, his hands under his head and looked up, at the top of the shuttle. Now it was simply a question of flying out of the atmosphere and aiming at the fleet. A simple task with relatively little natural danger. It all depended on the enemy now, and if they would waste missiles on a shuttle that was hard to see and harder to hit.

Torrence had fallen asleep. She rolled with the motions of the shuttle until she was up against Jefferson. He glanced out of the corner of his eye, looking at her, but made no move. He decided that he liked having her there.

Just as Jefferson was getting comfortable, the warning bell sounded and the pilot announced, "We are preparing to dock with the ship."

Torrence woke and sat up. She glanced at Jefferson and then at the others around them. "Sorry."

"For what?"

"Falling asleep like that."

"Don't worry about it." He shifted around, putting a little more space between them.

The shuttle slipped into the docking bay and the forward motion stopped. As it settled to the deck, Jefferson stood up. He stepped toward the ramp and waited as the docking bay was sealed and the air was pumped back into it. There was a servo whine and the ramp lowered. When Jefferson stepped out, a group of people dressed in white moved forward. Medical personnel coming to take care of the wounded.

Jefferson walked across the deck, stopped at the airlock, and waited until the hatch opened. Torrence stood behind him. He glanced at her.

"What's the plan now?" she asked.

He fingered the front of his uniform and said, "Ten minutes to shower and to change. Then we meet with Clemens on the bridge."

She grinned and said, "Shower alone?"

"If I didn't know you were kidding, I'd take you up on that. But then the shower would take more than ten minutes."

They ducked through the hatch and came out in a corridor. White lights burned in it, indicating that it was day on the ship. There were a few armed guards stationed along the corridor. Jefferson had never understood the rationale behind that, except as a reminder that they were on a military mission.

"Ten minutes," he said to Torrence.

"Ten minutes."

Jefferson turned and headed toward his cabin. He reached it, opened it, and then walked straight to the shower. He set his weapon on the desk and sat down in the chair. Kicking his boots off, he stood, stripped the tattered jumpsuit, and peeled himself out of the bulletproof and laser-resistant vest.

But before he could get into the shower, there was a tap at the hatch. Jefferson spun and stared at the hatch, but the tapping came again. Ignoring his nudity, he opened up and stepped back.

Garvey burst through the door. "I know what you did. It didn't fool me. Now I want to go down on the next deployment." He stopped and stared. "Ah . . ."

"I am not responsible for an equipment malfunction," said Jefferson.

Garvey looked at the naked man and then said, "I could, ah, come back later."

"No, Mr. Garvey, let's get this taken care of now."

"I don't know how you expect me to do my job when I am denied access to the story."

"Have you talked with the wounded?"

"No, but that's not the same thing. They're all soldiers and won't say anything. I want to be able to see . . ." He stared down and then shook his head. "This isn't working."

"What?"

"Colonel, I'll come back some other time."

Jefferson shrugged. "Suit yourself." As Garvey moved to the hatch, Jefferson stepped toward the alcove. But before he could get the water started, there was another tap at the hatch.

"Come on in," he shouted as he touched the switch to open the hatch.

Now Norris stepped through, looked at Jefferson, and said, "I see you're ready."

"I'm going to ignore that."

She moved toward him, looking as if she wanted to embrace him.

"No," said Jefferson. "I've got to get to the bridge in a few minutes."

"Later," she said, smiling.

"Courtney," said Jefferson. Then he stopped because he didn't know what he wanted to say. He shook his head. "Just get out of here."

"Yes, sir." That didn't bother her though. She grinned and said, "I'll return later."

Then, as she disappeared from the cabin, Jefferson moved into the tiny alcove. He turned on the water and stepped under it, turning so that it beat down on the back of his neck for a moment. Finally he turned and soaped himself quickly. Then he rinsed and stepped from the shower. Letting the cool air dry him, he padded into the other room. He pulled a clean uniform from the rack and put it on.

As he was zipping it up, there was a signal at the hatch. Opening it, he found Torrence there already. Her hair was still damp from the shower.

Slipping his feet into his boots, he said, "I'm ready. Let's go."

Together they left, walked down the corridor, and then entered the elevator. They rode up to the bridge, exited, and then waited until Clemens invited them forward.

"Give me a full report," said Jefferson as he moved forward.

Clemens launched into a discussion about the attacks on the fleet and his efforts to repel it. He mentioned the launch of missiles from the planet's surface and the two ships that had attacked him.

"Local ships?" asked Jefferson.

Clemens shrugged. "Both my intelligence people and yours failed to identify the vessels, they are Earth ships, of that we're sure. The configuration fits nothing that we've ever seen and we have nothing that matches it. That doesn't rule out the European Economic Community."

"There a reason that you keep bringing them into this?"

Clemens shrugged. "Rumblings before we left Earth. Just rumors that the Euro-Africa Economic Block is not happy with our expansion into this system, especially since we've frozen them out here."

"That wasn't included in any of my briefing packages," said Jefferson.

"Nor mine," said Clemens. "It was something that I picked up unofficially and mention only because it seems to be an interesting coincidence. The Euro group is unhappy and suddenly the aliens here are unhappy."

Jefferson nodded, taking it all in, and then changed the subject slightly. "I suppose that you're keeping a watch on the launch activity on that planet."

"Of course. And we're watching the surface of the planet below us as well. Nothing will sneak up on us."

Jefferson rubbed his chin. "What's this do to your support of our ground forces?"

"Nothing, unless we are engaged at the moment. We'll be within two hours of giving you all the support you need. At the very most."

"I'd hoped it would be faster than that."

"With no complications, it probably will be."

Jefferson nodded and said, "I'd like Captain Carter up here now. I want his assessment of the situation down below."

Clemens nodded and said, "I've asked for the same thing. He did tell me that all the human outposts have now been abandoned."

"All of them?"

"Our scans show no habitation except at the main city. Everyone has gotten out, all of them heading toward the city."

"That's not good."

Torrence spoke for the first time. "Carter indicate why the aliens have suddenly turned hostile?"

"Nothing," said Clemens. "He didn't even mention the Euros. That is an outgrowth of my intelligence function."

"We didn't initiate this, did we?" asked Jefferson. "It's not something our people started, is it?"

"I don't know," said Clemens. "Who knows how these things start? Hell, on old Earth wars were started over the most trivial of reasons."

"Because they were looking for an excuse to fight. There hasn't been any animosity between our two races."

"Well," said Clemens, "there's obviously something between them now. Every human outpost has now been eliminated."

"And we've been attacked," said Torrence.

"Do you have a plan, Colonel?"

"It would seem that the smart thing to do would be to

abandon the city as well. Evacuate all the civilians until we can get to the bottom of this."

"And take them where? We don't have the facilities aboard the ships. Too many of them and not enough life support. There's nothing, nowhere, to take them."

Jefferson nodded. "I was afraid you'd say something like that." He turned, looked at the screen that showed the blackness of space surrounding the ship. He stared at it, wishing that there was a solution out there.

"We could move them temporarily to the second planet," said Torrence.

"Hell, Vicky, that's just plain stupid. We're having trouble with the aliens here, what makes you think they'd be thrilled to see several thousand humans arrive there."

"Temporarily," she repeated.

"It stands to reason that anything happening here is done with the knowledge and approval of the aliens there. I think we could rule that out."

"We could ask," she said.

"No," said Clemens. "That telegraphs our weakened position. We can't ask because it could provoke an all-out assault on us and then they could mop up the city below at their leisure."

"So what do we do?" she asked.

"The only thing we can. Land the entire regiment near the city, secure it, protect it, and once that is done, we've some time to figure out solutions, even if it's bringing in colony ships and evacuating everyone."

"How long will that take?" asked Clemens.

"Preparations for the regiment and the deployment of them. A week, ten days. Setting up the secure bases, probably another two months."

"We could have the colony ships on the way."

Jefferson nodded and said, "But if we secure the area, then those ships won't be necessary."

"But it'll take two months from the time we decide to call for them. Maybe we should call now. We can always cancel them later."

Before Jefferson could respond, the commo operator turned. "Captain, I've just lost communications with the city."

"How so?"

"It's just like last night. Low-level electromagnetic radiation dampening the signals. We're unable to punch through it to them and reestablish contact."

"That's what happened to us," said Torrence.

And Jefferson knew the rest of it. After the contact was lost, the enemy attacked. In force.

"Looks like you don't have your week to ten days," said Clemens.

"Alert the battalion commanders. We'll be deploying a heavy landing force within the hour."

18

REARDON FELT A rage burn through him. He hated the people out in the streets creating flimsy barricades that would not turn back an attack of Boy Scouts. His head hurt and his stomach hurt and he was sick of the whole mess. It was an attitude that came on him suddenly, as he stood there, watching the frantic activity in front of him.

"This sucks," he said, and turned from the doorway.

"What's wrong with you?" asked Rachel.

"Don't be stupid." He waved a hand at the outside. "Look at them. Idiots. They're celebrating the arrival of the army but it won't do any good. Army'll either make everyone come in here or try to evacuate us all."

"You don't know that."

"I know enough."

She turned from the door and looked into the darkened room. "I want to go out to celebrate with them."

"Go!" snapped Reardon. "Celebrate. But I'll tell you one thing. It's early for a celebration."

"Why?"

"Because the army isn't here yet. We've some communication that claims the army is close, but I don't see them. I don't see anything that suggests they're near."

She moved to the door and then stopped. The celebration had suddenly slowed. There was still some yelling, still some whistling, but it had faded considerably. A few people were standing around, looking confused.

"What's going on out there?" she asked.

The question enraged Reardon. He didn't know why it did, only that the sound of her voice and the stupidity of the question irritated him. Maybe it was from having to drag her around for several days, saving her from the aliens. Maybe it was her belief that he would somehow have answers to questions when she had just as much information about it as he did. He whirled on her and swung, but missed her on purpose. Instead he struck the wall near her.

"What . . . ?"

"Just shut up," roared Reardon. "Shut up for two minutes. That's all I ask."

"I'll do better," she said. "I'll get out."

Reardon watched her go, not sure why he was so angry. She had done nothing wrong. It was just that she was there, talking when she should have been quiet.

Reardon moved to the doorway and looked out on the shouting, screaming, confused crowd. Some of the people were yanking at the barricades, tearing them down in anger. Others, just as intent, were trying to put them back up.

Before he had a chance to digest that, a machine gun opened fire. A distant rattling of fire. That galvanized the people in the street. They froze, turning to face the sound. One man raised his hand to shade his eyes. Another climbed on top of a barricade, trying to see over the debris in the street.

"They're coming!" a woman screamed. "They're *coming*!"

"Where's the army?" asked a man.

"Someone sound the warning," ordered Jackson.

"Can you see them?" asked Goswell.

The machine gun fell silent for a moment, and then started up again, joined by another and then another. There was an explosion off somewhere in the city. A quiet dull pop as the first of the mortars began to fall.

And as that happened, a woman began to scream, her voice rising like the wail of a siren.

* * *

Jefferson stood at the head of the table and looked at the staff officers seated around it. He had assembled them all, including the company commanders who had yet to deploy. There were seven people including Torrence. She sat to one side, out of the way, listening.

"It seems that we don't have much time," said Jefferson. "The aliens have pushed forward their timetable, whatever it might be, and we must respond."

"How do we know that?"

Jefferson looked at Peyton, the operations officer. "Before the assaults on Torrence last night, the aliens created a low-level screen of radiation that prevented communications from the inside of it. In the last few minutes, such a screen was erected around the last human stronghold. It is our belief that the city if not already under attack will be shortly."

"Shit," said Carter.

"My feelings exactly."

"We have any idea of what in the hell is going on?" asked Peyton.

"Captain Carter?" said Jefferson.

Carter stood up and then shook his head. "I find myself in the position of knowing a few facts, but none of them mean much."

"Elaborate."

Carter shrugged. "The vessels that attacked us a few hours ago are from the Euro-Africa Economic Block."

"Oh, hell," said Jefferson, "we already have discussed that. No state of war exists between us and the Euro-Africans," he said. "Why would they attack us?"

Carter stroked his chin and said, "It might be that our shot across their bow was interpreted as a hostile act. Since they had not fired on us, they responded to our warning shot as a hostile act."

"I would like something a little more solid than your speculations."

"Yes, sir. We believe that the low-level jamming system being employed by the aliens is a derivative of a device originally designed and used by the Soviets."

"You now telling me there is Soviet involvement?"

"No, sir. The technology was originated by the Soviets, but we think it has been enhanced by the Euro-Africans and is being sold throughout the galaxy."

"Crap," said Jefferson. "And this is getting us nowhere. What is happening on the ground? Now."

Carter turned toward the projection screen. A flat map of the city and surrounding territory was displayed there. Carter stepped closer and then shook his head. "I've gotten no new input for the last hour or so."

Jefferson nodded and studied the map. According to what they knew, the city sat on a huge plain that started at the shoreline, off a large, shallow, and protected bay. The land rose slowly, toward some fairly short mountains no more than two thousand feet high. There was a single wide river that looped through the center of the city effectively dividing it in two. All the approaches to the city were open. Attackers would have to cross a lot of open ground to get at the humans.

Peyton said, "Colonel, the best landing sites, using our shuttles, are here, northeast of the city."

"Pods?"

Peyton shrugged. "If you want to use them, then we can put them down anywhere. I'd advise shuttles only because the landing force will have some protection coming down and we can put a battalion down at once without having to rally. There is the open ground available to do it."

"But we can only deploy one battalion at a time that way," said Torrence.

"Does that matter?"

Jefferson, still studying the map, said, "I don't think so. But we might want to designate two or three landing zones."

"No problem. There is a place east of the city, maybe a klick out, that is perfect."

Jefferson waved a hand. "This is getting us nowhere. I want a plan for deploying the regiment to the city and I want it in thirty minutes. I want all companies standing by for deployment, Companies A through D for the First Tactical Battalion. Headquarters company will remain here to oversee the deployment. I want the first shuttles launched inside an hour. Captain Carter, I want an intelligence update provided for each of the company commanders and I want an overall update for me, and I want that in twenty minutes. Have I forgotten anything?"

"Captain Sinclair's makeshift battalion on the ground already," said Torrence.

"Contact her and have her make arrangements to move her people toward the city using the floaters. She is not to engage the enemy. She will avoid a fight until we get everyone else on the ground. Her mission is to support us if and when we need it."

"Yes, sir."

"Questions?"

"Will the headquarters company be deploying at all?"

Jefferson turned and looked into Norris's blue eyes. He shook his head, thinking that the problem of ordering her into combat had come up already. Should he deploy them or not? The answer was easy. Headquarters should remain on the ship where they could coordinate everything on the ground. Pure and simple. And even with that he wondered if Norris's presence had colored the decision. He decided not.

"Headquarters will remain in down-link communications with the deployed forces but the personnel will remain on the ship."

"Yes, sir."

"Let's get at it," said Jefferson. "I want the First Battalion on the ground inside an hour."

As the staff officers filed out of the conference room, Torrence hung back. When they were alone, she asked, "We both going to deploy?"

"Nope. I want you to remain here to coordinate the activities."

"That's the job of the commander," said she.

"Nope. Job of the commander is to do what he sees fit. Job of the executive officer is to stay on board and coordinate."

"You're keeping me out of the fight."

Jefferson nodded and then grinned. Again he wondered if he was issuing orders to protect someone. Again he decided that the logic of the situation dictated his decisions. He wasn't unconsciously protecting anyone.

"If," he said, still grinning, "I get killed down there, then you can come down to take over, telling your replacement to stay up here to coordinate."

"Don't talk like that," she said.

"Why not?"

"Because these jokes have a way of coming true. You don't believe you're going to get killed but you joke about it and the next thing I know, they're zipping you into a body bag."

"Thank you very much," said Jefferson. "I certainly appreciate having the reality of the situation thrust into my face just before a deployment."

"That's not what I meant."

"Doesn't matter," said Jefferson, waving a hand. He moved toward the hatch.

"You think it's a good idea for you to go down?"

"I think it's necessary. The commander shouldn't order the troops to do something he wouldn't do himself."

"But you've already proven that," she said.

"Vicky, it doesn't matter. If the regiment deploys, I should deploy with it. Hell, every other officer could stay on the ship, as long as I go down. It's important that the troops see me on the ground with them."

They moved out into the corridor then. There were people hurrying along it. Men and women from the First Battalion, trying to get ready for the deployment. The crew of the ship was moving too. Everyone preparing.

Norris was standing near the door. She watched as Jefferson and Torrence came out, hesitated, and then stepped forward. "Can I talk to you for a minute, Colonel?"

"Certainly." He turned toward Torrence. "I'll see you one more time before we launch."

Torrence stood there for a moment, looking at Norris and then at Jefferson. "Just be careful," she said. And then she turned, hurrying away.

"What can I do for you, Courtney?" asked Jefferson.

She glanced right and then left, but there were too many people around. Glancing up, she said, "I think I should go down to the planet's surface."

"No reason for it."

"You're going," she said.

"That's different. The supply officer has no need to land with the strike force. Staff officers have to stay here."

"Will I have a chance to see you . . . alone, before the deployment?"

Jefferson stood still for a moment and then shook his head. "No time."

For a moment she didn't say a word but finally mumbled, "I understand." She turned and hurried up the corridor.

Jefferson headed toward his quarters. He stopped at the hatch and looked behind him. The pace seemed to have increased. The people were walking faster. A few were trotting, trying to get things accomplished. The noise level had also increased. The people were talking faster and louder than normal. The excitement of the deployment was beginning to affect everyone.

He entered his cabin and stripped the jumpsuit he wore. From the alcove, he took the bulletproof vest and donned it. He then put on socks, a camouflaged jumpsuit, boots, and finally a pistol belt that held his equipment, which included a knife with a laser-honed blade. The combat uniform contained no rank insignia and looked just like that worn by every other soldier. He didn't want anything that would set him apart and make him a target.

Picking up his weapon, he took a final look around the cabin. Nothing spectacular about it. A cot, a desk, and the alcove for the shower. But it was his cabin. His home. It was all he had and for the moment he didn't want to leave it.

Then, shaking his head, he stepped through the hatch and joined the stream of people heading toward the shuttle bay. Launch was getting closer.

19

CARTER CAUGHT JEFFERSON at the hatch that led out into the shuttle bay. He stepped up to him and said, "I've got the information that you asked for, Colonel."

Jefferson switched his laser rifle to his left hand and said, "Let me have it."

"Long-range scans and radar searches provided us with little data due to the jamming interference . . ."

"I don't want to hear the excuses, I want the data," snapped Jefferson.

"They are not excuses. They are reasons for the poor quality of the information."

"Get on with it."

"The enemy aliens are forming on the northern side of the city. There seem to be blocking forces of company strength on the south and on the east, but they're spread thin."

"Size of the main body?"

"I don't know, sir. We estimate that it is regimental strength, maybe as large as fifteen hundred individuals or maybe a little less."

"Outnumbered by the people in the city."

"Yes, sir. But then most of the people in the city are not

combatants. And none of them have military training. A guy with a gun isn't a soldier. He's a guy with a gun."

"But he can kill a soldier," said Jefferson.

"The point is, sir, that even though there are more humans than that in the city, a well-trained military force will have no trouble overrunning them."

"There a time frame for that?"

"Given what Major Torrence told me, I would suspect that the attacks will begin within an hour of the first low frequency masking, meaning that they should have begun by now."

"We're going down into a hot environment?" asked Jefferson.

Carter shrugged. "That depends on the enemy and on the landing zones, but I doubt that the enemy will be looking for you."

"Let's hope not. Anything else?"

"No, sir. Without the capability to penetrate the jamming dome, I can only guess and your guess is as good as mine."

"Then wish me luck."

"Good luck, Colonel."

"I'll be in touch." Before he could move, Garvey appeared down the corridor. Jefferson pretended he didn't see the reporter but said to Carter, "You keep that man away from me." With that he stepped through the hatch and into the shuttle bay.

The dropping of the mortars started the panic. People fled the barricade, running toward the buildings, hoping for safety inside them. The distant pops of the weapons firing came closer as the enemy advanced. The rounds, falling on the outskirts of the city, began walking, slowly, toward the interior. Smoke from the fires began to rise. A thick black smoke that marked the progress of the enemy's weapons.

Some of the men began to filter back into the streets, manning the barricades. First they stood there, lined up behind the broken furniture, the overturned cars, and the boxes and sacks of food and meal. They surveyed the city in front of them, searching for signs that the aliens were coming. And then, one by one, they began to work at rebuilding the walls ruined in the celebration. They piled the debris higher and thicker, giving themselves some real protection from the enemy bullets.

Women joined the men. All were armed but there was no consistency in the arms. Only the police, a self-appointed, self-regulated force that had done more harm than good, had similar weapons. Each of the men and women had a laser pistol and an assault rifle. The rifles all used the same kind of ammo. One man could give a magazine to a woman and she could use that ammo in her weapon.

But the rest of the people had whatever they had brought with them, or what they had bought once they had gotten to the planet. They had laser rifles and slug throwers. There were shotguns and pistols and a few scattered grenade launchers. Most of the weapons were designed more as hunting tools than instruments of defense. No one expected the locals to turn hostile and to attack.

Reardon, still feeling angry with everything, walked out into the bright sunlight shining down on the street. He blinked at it and then moved to the barricade, siding along it until he found a good place near the left side of it. There was a stone building against his shoulder. No way for the enemy to get behind him easily. He glanced at the laser rifle in his hands. It was fully charged and ready to go.

The sounds of the fighting came closer. Over the top of the barricade, Reardon could see the mortar rounds detonating. Explosions with black smoke and flashes of fire. Debris was thrown up into the air and rained back with a rattling of its own. Dust drifted on the light breeze.

Machine guns supported the mortars. The distant hammering was closer now. An occasional round snapped through the air over them. Men and women dived for cover. One man began to scream and threw away his rifle. He ran toward a building, bounced off a locked door, and then leapt through a window, disappearing.

"Asshole," muttered Reardon.

Rachel walked up behind him then. She was moving slowly, staying close to the building, and was hunched over like the soldiers in a hundred war movies. She reached him and slipped to one knee. In her right hand she held an old automatic pistol.

"Where should I be?"

"Inside, out of the line of fire."

"Bullshit."

Reardon glanced at her. She'd done well enough as they had worked to get from the forest into the city, but there had been no fighting then. Just walking through the trees and staying out of sight.

"You know how to use that?" he asked.

"Bullets come out of this end when I pull the trigger here. I point this end at the enemy."

"Fire low," said Reardon.

"Why?"

"Because everyone tends to fire high when the shooting starts. If you try to shoot low, the bullets should hit the enemy about chest high."

She moved forward, stepped up on a wooden box, and peeked over the top of the barricade. There was a crash and she jumped down, turning her back.

"Wasn't close," said Reardon, but he'd ducked too. Shrapnel rattled against the barricade.

He stood up and looked over the top of the barricade. A mortar crashed through the roof of a building and blew out the door and windows with a muffled thud. The glass exploded into the street, shattering and then sparkling like a million diamonds thrown by the hand of a giant.

And then the street in front of him filled with the aliens. Hundreds of them pouring into the center of the city, running forward, filtered by the buildings. Firing erupted behind them. Machine guns and then lasers. Beams of light, faded by the bright sun, flashed overhead. Tracers hit the barricade and bounced upward, tumbling. Others snapped by to slam into the buildings, ricocheting.

Reardon felt the tug of déjà vu. He remembered standing in his camp as the aliens hit it, though that was at night. He straightened and squeezed off a short burst but didn't aim it. He just fired and ducked. Not like in the movies where the hero stands tall, bullets flashing all around him, and he calmly shoots down the attacking hordes.

Rounds struck just overhead, smashing into the debris. Bits of it were torn loose and rained down on him. Angered, he leapt up again, but this time looked down at the enemy. Dozens

of them running and firing. Reardon aimed a shot at the center
of the mass and saw a creature tumble to the street rolling
over. Two of its fellows tripped on its body and they too went
down. One failed to get up but the other struggled to its knees.
Reardon fired at it, missed it, but there were so many of the
aliens attacking that he hit another. And then another.

Now most of the people at the barricade were firing. Some
of them held their weapons over their heads and pulled the
triggers hoping for the best. Others were popping up, firing,
and dropping back down. Shooting into the mass of aliens.

A woman was hit as she tried to squeeze off a round. The
bullet smashed into her forehead and peeled back part of the
scalp. She shrieked in surprise and pain, grabbed at the wound,
and fell straight to the rear landing flat on her back. Her feet
drummed on the pavement as her blood pumped from the
wound until the ground around her was crimson and she had
died.

There was another scream behind the barricade and a man
dropped to the street. A second man followed, hit in the chest.
He tried to sit up and then folded over, dying quietly.

Reardon stood and fired again, swinging his laser in a short
arc. Four aliens went down. Others turned, firing at Reardon,
trying to kill him. He dived to the left, up against the building
as the bullets slammed into the barricade. Over the sounds of
the yelling and the firing, he could hear the rounds striking the
debris. Bits of it were kicked up, into the air, creating a small,
swirling cloud.

He wiped the sweat on his shirtsleeve, unaware of the sun or
the heat or the noise. Suddenly he was lost in a vacuum where
there was no one but him and the aliens. Everything else was
lost and it was like standing in a long dark tunnel with the
aliens in the sun at the far end. He popped up, fired, ducked,
and then went through it again. Firing, firing, firing.

All around him the battle took on the qualities of a silent
movie. No one said a word. He could see their lips moving but
heard nothing from them. People toppled to the street. Blood
splashed and ran into the gutters. Wounded tried to escape the
barricade. Others sat with their hands pressed to their bodies,
their fingers bloody, their clothes soaked.

Reardon stood slowly, aimed, and saw another of the aliens

fall to the street. He stood there then, bullets singing around him, bouncing off the walls, the barricade, flashing over his head, and calmly began to kill the enemy. He stood tall, just like the invulnerable heroes of the afternoon movies, killing the enemy. He fired short bursts, aimed them carefully. Aim, fire, aim, fire, aim, fire. The enemy soldiers fell.

And then the mortars came back, crashing into the buildings around them. There were explosions, debris blown out into the street. Fires sprang up and black smoke poured out and up, into the sun-bright sky.

But the humans at the barricade were cheering then. As the mortars fell, destroying more of the city, the attacking aliens were retreating, leaving their dead and wounded sprawled in the street. Reardon crawled to the top of the barricade and began to systematically shoot the wounded. One shot at the head of each moaning, writhing alien.

Rachel was up next to him, tugging at him. "Stop it. Stop it. The battle's over."

But Reardon kept at it, shooting at the bodies of those he suspected still lived, trying to kill every alien left behind. He kept shooting until the tunnel expanded and the light filtered in and he realized that he had survived the first assault.

He stopped shooting and looked at the scene. A hundred aliens were sprawled in the street that was wet with their blood. A building close to them burned, the flames leaping skyward. There was a stench in the air that he couldn't identify. Burning flesh or hot blood or something like that. A butcher yard at high noon on the hottest day of the year. A sickening odor that burned through to the brain.

Reardon turned and slipped down the barricade until he was sitting with his feet on the ground, his back to the barricade. The wounded humans had been dragged to cover, the only evidence of them the crimson stains left behind. The dead lay where they had fallen. Mangled bodies with holes ripped in them and arms and legs ripped from them. Reardon had never known the damage a bullet could do to the human body. He was used to seeing the tidy corpses produced by television and movies. Real dead bodies were anything but tidy.

"We did it," said Rachel then. "We beat them back."

"Sure," said Reardon.

"We've won and without the help of the army."

Realizing that he was going to sound just like a pretend soldier in a cliché-riddled movie, he said, "Don't worry. They'll be back."

Jefferson moved across the deck, to where the shuttle waited. Lined up next to the ramp were the soldiers who were to land on it. A lieutenant inspected them, followed by a sergeant. They were making sure that each soldier had his or her weapon ready for the fight and that each carried a share of the squad equipment that included extra ammo for the grenadiers, battery packs for the squad weapons, and first-aid gear. When they were satisfied that everyone carried everything that was needed, the sergeant led the soldiers onto the shuttle.

"I'll be riding down with you, Lieutenant," said Jefferson as he approached.

"Yes, sir." The lieutenant was quiet for a moment and then asked, "Intell updates."

"Given to me just moments earlier, Lieutenant . . . ?

"Slovik, sir. Erick Slovik."

"I thought I knew my officers."

"Yes, sir. I was attached to the regiment just prior to sailing and was instructed to report directly to Major James. She didn't get around to introducing me to you."

"Well, Slovik, board the shuttle. We have work to do."

"Yes, sir."

As Slovik trotted up the ramp, Jefferson turned. There were a dozen people standing behind the glass of the shuttle bay's control booth. Torrence stood in the crowd, as did Carter and a couple of the other officers who would deploy later. Only Torrence seemed to be watching him. He lifted a hand and waved and saw her nod in response. He then turned and walked up the ramp. As soon as he was inside, the loadmaster touched a button and the ramp lifted into place, sealing them in.

The soldiers were spread out on both sides of the shuttle, sitting on the soft deck and leaning against the padding of the fuselage. Each held a weapon and each looked ready for the coming fight.

The shuttle vibrated and began to roll toward the hatch that would allow it to drop into space. As it did, Jefferson crouched in the center of it and looked into the faces of his soldiers. He waited until they suddenly dropped, the shuttle now in space. The engines fired briefly and they began the long descending flight.

Crouching there, in the center of the group like a football coach trying to inspire his team before the big game, he looked into the faces of the people and told them that they didn't know if the enemy was attacking the city or not. "The indications are that the enemy was on the move.

"On the ground," said Jefferson, "we form at the rally points and then move into the city."

"These aliens are around?" asked one of the women.

"As far as we know, they are either about to attack, or are in the process of attacking. The aliens are about. We have to be careful."

"Rules of engagement?" asked a man.

"Simple. If you see an alien, kill it." Jefferson grinned. "That doesn't mean opening fire if you're going to expose yourself or your fellows to attack. We have to use good tactics, but I don't want someone to fail to shoot if a target presents itself."

"Roger that, Colonel," shouted someone in the rear.

"Let's just be careful. Remember your training. Let's not have anyone killed by making a stupid mistake."

Jefferson moved back and sat down. He looked at his weapon. He looked at the people around him. He looked at the bulkhead of the shuttle and he looked at the deck under him. There wasn't much to see, but that was all there was.

And then the warning bell was sounding and Jefferson could hear the roar of the engines as they passed through the atmosphere. He stood up and moved to the single window on the left side of the fuselage. They were getting close.

He sat down as the warning bell rang again. The loadmaster was moving through the cabin saying, "Coming up on landing. Coming up on landing."

Jefferson turned and faced the ramp. The soldiers near him shifted around until they were all ready to go. Jefferson looked up at the loadmaster. "Any reports from the pilots?"

"No, sir. They say that the touchdown point is clear of aliens."

"How long?"

"Two minutes."

Jefferson glanced at the soldiers. They were getting nervous and he understood that. Moving into a hostile environment, the enemy around somewhere and no one knew where. "Let's get ready," he said.

The nose of the shuttle came up then and they slowed suddenly. Jefferson felt the pressure pushing down on him, trying to knock him over. But just as suddenly, the pressure was gone. They bounced once and then rolled to a quick stop.

As that happened, the loadmaster was lowering the ramp. He stood, his thumb pressing the button, standing back out of the way. As the top of the ramp folded down and they could see out onto the landscape, he was yelling, "Get out! Get on out! Move it!"

The instant the ramp was in place, Jefferson sprinted down it. He leapt to one side and scrambled clear. He crouched in the long grass, glanced around to make sure that he was not surrounded by aliens, and then faced toward the city. In moments, the shuttle was empty and rolling forward to take off. Jefferson closed his eyes against the blowing dust kicked up by the shuttle's engines.

And then the shuttle was gone, as were those that had landed with it. The soldiers were up and moving, heading toward the city with one officer running off, out in front as the point. He was followed by three soldiers trying to catch him. Over the city there was a cloud of black smoke. A huge cloud that indicated things were burning there.

"Colonel?" said Slovik.

"Move it out. Get flankers out and a squad for a rear guard."

"We're not going to hold the landing zone?"

"We're going to push into the city."

"Yes, sir."

Jefferson was now hurrying forward, toward the point. He looked again at the smoke and hoped that they weren't too late. At the moment, it didn't look good.

20

As soon as the shuttles dropped out of sight and it was announced that all were in perfect flight, Torrence ran from the control room. She hurried along the corridor to the elevator, and entered. Just as the doors were sliding closed, Norris appeared, stuck an arm in so that doors would open again, and then entered. The car began to move.

"Where you going, Major?"

"To the bridge."

"Ah. Mind if I tag along?"

Torrence shrugged and then asked, "There a good reason for you going up there?"

"I want to know what the regiment is doing."

The elevator stopped and the doors opened. Torrence stood there for an instant and then asked, "Isn't there something you should be doing in supply?"

"Like what?"

"Your job," said Torrence.

"That's forms to fill out, records to keep, and equipment to count. There are sergeants to oversee the privates doing that. My job is to sign for everything and take responsibility if there is a discrepancy in supply."

"I'd want to make sure that my NCOs weren't stealing me blind," said Torrence.

"And what would they do with the stuff. There's no black market here on the ships."

"I would prefer that you were down in supply in case you're needed there."

"Is that an order?"

Torrence shrugged. "I had hoped that it wouldn't be necessary for me to make it one but I will."

Norris stood there, her arms folded, and glared at Torrence. "Yes, ma'am. I'll rush right back down there and make sure that none of the equipment is getting away."

There wasn't anything for Torrence to say to that. She could mention that Norris was only a first lieutenant and that orders were orders, but that would do no good. Instead, she ignored the attitude and stepped out onto the bridge.

As soon as the doors slipped closed, Torrence moved toward the center of the bridge where Clemens sat watching the view screen in front of him. "Anything yet?"

He turned and then shook his head. "I'd thought you'd want to be in the shuttle bay."

"There's a dozen officers down there to handle that. I'm the fifth wheel." As she said it she realized that it was the argument that Norris had just given her. She grinned. "If I'm not in the way, I think I'll be more valuable here. I'll get the information faster and can make the changes needed."

"I'm afraid there isn't much information." Clemens snapped his fingers. "Jenkins, give me a view of the shuttles."

The picture on the screen changed abruptly. Suddenly it was black with points of light and the formation of shuttles in the center of it. They were diving down, toward the planet's surface, which was a small smudge in the bottom right corner.

"You see," he said. "Nothing yet."

"Commo with the planet's surface?"

"Nothing. We've still got the blackout situation."

"Jesus."

Clemens said, "That's a good sign. If they'd overrun the city, they'd probably have turned off the jamming equipment. Since they haven't, I would guess that there are still survivors down there."

Torrence moved to the right and sat down in one of the vacant chairs. She gripped the arms as the shuttles hit the atmosphere and began to rocket down. She sat quietly as they maneuvered in the atmosphere. They had limited flight capability and if the aliens launched any missiles, they would have a hard time evading them. But no missiles were launched as the shuttles fell toward the ground.

Torrence sat on the edge of the chair, watching the changing scene, her fingers digging into the soft material of the chair. As the shuttles flared, she held her breath, waiting for an ambush to spring, but none came. Instead the shuttles rolled safely to a halt and the soldiers in them sprang out. They swarmed over the field, forming into a strung-out unit with a group running forward as the point.

The commo from the ground was broken, spotty, but it did get through. "Shuttles down and unloaded. No enemy action."

"Roger. Take off now."

"On the go."

Clemens turned and said, "They're just outside the dome of interference."

Even in the air-conditioned comfort of the ship, Torrence found herself sweating. Now she understood why Jefferson had insisted on going down with the regiment. It was unnerving to be sitting there, watching the war. She wanted to get into the action, not because she hungered for glory but because it was her regiment in the fight. Her friends were down there, about to enter battle while she sat there, comfortable and safe, watching them.

"Commo's going," said Jenkins. "I'm only picking up one word in five."

Torrence turned. "You have a source for the jamming located?"

"No, ma'am. Problem is that the jamming camouflages itself. There are two points where it is stronger than others and those might be the transmitting locations or it might be overlaps of some kind. It's deceptive."

"Captain," said Torrence. "Can we bomb those points?"

Clemens was quiet for a moment and then said, "I don't see why not." He spun in his chair and said, "Targeting, I want the two strong points located and attacked."

"Yes, sir."

"Jenkins, give them the plotting information."

"Aye, sir."

Torrence stood up and moved forward, Quietly, under her breath, she said, "Good luck, Dave."

The rumble of shuttle engines split the air over the city. Reardon heard them and for a moment thought that it was thunder from the building clouds south of the city. Then to the north and east he saw a flash of light and the tiny shape of the distant shuttle.

"Army's here," he muttered and then turned to face the other people. Almost none of them had looked up. They were concentrating on the wounded and the aliens and the streets in front of them.

Reardon slipped from his position and moved toward Rachel. She sat on the sidewalk, her back to a building. In her hands was the rifle she had used. She was staring at the sidewalk, her face blank.

"Army's coming," he said.

"How do you know?"

He hitchhiked a thumb over his shoulder and said, "Shuttle landing. Saw it."

"Not much help in a shuttle," she said.

Reardon grinned and asked, "You ever heard of pathfinders? A couple of them land to locate the best LZ and the rest of the force follows in a few minutes."

From behind them came a shout. "Here they come again."

Firing erupted all around them. Reardon glanced at the center of the barricade and then stepped up to his position. He glanced over the top and saw the aliens filtering into the street again, but this time there were creatures up on the flat roofs supporting the attack with machine-gun fire. The rounds snapped overhead.

"They're coming," said Reardon.

Rachel nodded but didn't move for a moment. She sat there, as if stunned by the information. Finally she looked at him and climbed to her feet.

Reardon slipped to the left so that his shoulder was against the wall of the building. His head was below the level of the barricade. Bullets from the machine guns ripped at the top of it and slammed into the wall near him. He realized that the machine gunners were the most dangerous threat. They could keep the defenders pinned down, unable to repulse the attack until the aliens swarmed up the barricade and began a hand-to-hand fight that they would win. They had the numbers.

Reardon leaned forward, almost as if trying to stretch out on the barricade. He wiggled forward until he could see the edge of the buildings far in front of him. The machine guns there kept working, firing into the street. By slipping right or left or forward, he could see the gun crews. Ignoring the flying bullets and the onrushing aliens, he aimed at the gunner sitting behind his weapon.

He ducked down once, closed his eyes briefly, and then opened them. He took a breath, held it, and fired a short burst. The beam stabbed out and struck the gunner. He fell back as if he had suddenly gone to sleep.

Another alien leapt to take his place but before the creature could even aim the weapon, Reardon killed him. And then for good measure, he shot the assistant gunner. The enemy slumped forward and toppled from the roof.

Still he ignored the aliens in the street and concentrated on the machine guns on the roof. He fired at another, missed, and was rewarded as that gun targeted him. The slugs flipped debris down on him and ricocheted off the walls behind him. Once he was clipped by a chip of stone. That stung but it didn't bother him much.

Now Rachel was up near him. She had tried to get up so that she could fire into the street, but the machine-gun fire was too heavy. Instead, she began to shoot at the creatures on the roofs. Others followed that lead until the machine gunners were forced to fall back or get killed.

As that happened, Reardon and a dozen others scrambled higher on the barricade and began to fire at the aliens in the street. He shot, ducked, popped up, and fired again. He didn't wait to see the results. Just like the first time, the enemy was jammed close together. A shot into that mass provided him with a hit. The important thing was to keep the firing going.

The aliens sensed the folly of the new attack. Without a clear command, they turned and retreated again, leaving the dead and dying behind them. They ran back or just dived into the broken-out windows of the buildings, taking whatever cover they could find. Once inside, they began to snipe at the men and women on the barricades.

The nature of the battle changed then. It was the two sides, separated by a hundred yards, shooting at shadows and movement, hoping to hit one of the enemy. Everyone firing as fast as he or she could pull the trigger.

Reardon slipped down the barricade toward the street and said quietly to Rachel. "We don't have an endless supply of ammo and it takes a while to recharge a laser."

"So what?"

"So if the army doesn't get here soon we'll run out of ammo and the aliens will be able to walk right up to us because all we can do is throw rocks."

"The army will get here."

"I hope so."

They had been on the move for only ten minutes when the sounds of heavy firing drifted to them. The column halted for the moment and Jefferson moved forward to the point. The men and women crouched there, on a slight rise. Below them the city was spread out, but now it looked like the ruin of an ancient civilization. There was no sign of life on the outer edges of it. No movement. No color. Clouds of black smoke hung over it, drifting slowly out to sea. The firing came from farther away, deeper in the city.

Using his binoculars, Jefferson surveyed the scene but the only change was that the buildings were closer and the black clouds thicker. Even with the image-enhancing capabilities of the binoculars, there was nothing to see. He needed to either be higher so that he could look down into the center, or he needed to be closer.

He slipped to the rear and found the commo people, but their communications with the fleet was now gone. The jamming umbrella extended out and covered them. Jefferson shrugged at the news and told the people, "Keep trying."

Moving back toward the point, he ordered the column to move on. The point crossed the ridge and dipped down to the flat plain that led right up to the edge of the city. Jefferson expected the aliens to open fire at any moment, but they were apparently unaware that his soldiers were close to them.

Slowly, keeping low and to the little cover available, the battalion moved across the open plain. He felt the heat of the sun on his back, felt the sweat dripping, and the eyes of the enemy on him. He was sure that they had spotted them and would open fire at any moment. But it didn't happen and the walls of the city loomed larger as they got closer.

Keeping low and now running, the soldiers on the point made it to the wall. Jefferson was there a moment later, and strung out behind him was the rest of the column.

"No doors, Colonel," said a man.

Jefferson looked right and left and saw that the wall was a blank face. But it was only eight feet high. Not much of a barrier for trained men and women in good physical condition.

"Go on over it," said Jefferson.

"Sir?"

"Over the top. Let's go."

One man slung his weapon and leapt up, grabbing the top of the wall. He hauled himself up so that his eyes were above the top of the wall. Seeing that it was clear on the other side, he climbed on up and rolled out, onto the top. He glanced to the interior and then looked back down. "It's clear here."

Jefferson waved his hand and the battalion came closer, bunching up in the shadow of the wall. But just as quickly, the men and women began to scramble up, over it. Jefferson watched for a moment, saw that it was going smoothly, and then climbed. He found himself on the roof of a low building, the streets in front of him empty except for rubble. Rocks and bricks and abandoned goods were scattered. But no people.

Jefferson slipped along the rooftop until he came to the far edge. He knelt there, looking down, into the street. From the center of the city came the sounds of firing, but it was no longer as heavy as it had been.

Jefferson returned to the wall and whispered, "I want all company commanders up here at once." He then turned and faced the center of the city.

A moment later three men and one woman joined him. He glanced at them. All were young, slender, and all had dark hair. It was almost as if they all had been cut from the same mold. The woman was almost as big as the men but her features were softer, more delicate. She could easily have been the sister of the men.

Major Marsel joined them. He sat down and waited for instructions. He wasn't thrilled with having Jefferson assuming command, but there was nothing he could do about it.

"I want each company commander to take command of his or her company and move them through the streets toward the center of the city. We'll be separated by no more than one block and if any one company is attacked, the others will move to support it. Questions?"

"Point?"

"One platoon in the center, leading the way."

"Commo is out," said one man.

"I know. We'll stay in physical contact with one another."

There was a burst of heavy firing and that died away. Everyone turned and looked toward it. The woman said, "Maybe we're too late."

"No," said Jefferson. "The jamming is still going on. If they had captured or killed everyone, that jamming would have stopped." He glanced at the men and women and said, "If there is nothing else, get back to your companies. We move in five minutes."

"Yes, sir," said one of them.

Jefferson grabbed the shoulder of one of the men and said, "I'll be with your company. I want to move with the point."

"Yes, sir." He looked disappointed.

Jefferson moved to the edge of the roof, looked down into the street, and then slipped around so that he could drop down. He landed hard and fell back, landing on his butt. No one laughed.

Getting up, Jefferson said, "Let's get going."

The platoon formed around him and he began to move along the street, using the walls of the buildings for cover. One squad ran across the street and was moving along the structures there. They came to an intersection. Three soldiers sprinted across it and took up firing positions. But there were no aliens around it and the rest of the platoon crossed at a jog.

They moved on, not bothering with clearing the buildings around him. Everything looked to be deserted. The glass of the windows was broken and lying in the street and the sidewalk sparkling in the sun. Doors had been blown open or broken down. There was black on the walls of some of the buildings showing where fires had burned. But there was no evidence of fighting there. No pock marks on the walls from bullets, no scorch marks from lasers, and no craters from mortars. This section of the city had been abandoned before the enemy arrived.

At the next intersection, they halted. Jefferson slipped forward and peeked down the streets. Still there was no movement and no sound. Just the rattling of distant fire, filtered by the buildings and echoing from the stone. The smoke still hung over the city.

"Colonel?"

"We press on," said Jefferson. He pointed at three soldiers. Again they ran across the street and again no one fired at them. The platoon and then the company began moving then.

"We are prepared to fire," said the targeting officer.

"Then do it," said Torrence. "You don't have to wait for permission."

"On my ship, Major, they do have to wait," advised Clemens. Then, to the targeting officer, he said, "You have a problem there?"

"Yes, Captain. We don't know the exact distribution of Colonel Jefferson's troops. If we fire blindly we may kill or injure some of them."

"We need communications with the ground," said Torrence. "Can't you limit the destructive area of your weapons?"

"Of course, but we don't even have a target. A solid target. We have areas of intense signal activity but that could mean nothing at all."

"Put up the map," said Torrence.

Jenkins looked at Clemens who nodded. "Screen to map."

Pointing, Torrence said, "This area here is the landing zone for the shuttles?"

"As confirmed by our people," said Clemens.

"Colonel Jefferson's line of march would be directly to the city."

"Of course."

"Now display the areas of signal strength."

The map changed to show the dome of jamming including the two areas of strength. Torrence moved closer to the screen and then pointed at it.

"See," she demanded, "it's nowhere near Colonel Jefferson's line of march."

"I don't like firing blind," said Clemens. "Even if you're right about Jefferson's location, we don't know where the civilians are. Signal strength could mark their strongholds, the enemy feeling that most communications would come from there."

Torrence stood there silently for a moment and understood why Jefferson had not ordered them to try to penetrate the shield. They'd have to attack it blind and they didn't know who or what lay under it.

"I want Captain Carter up here," she said.

"Have the captain report to the bridge," said Clemens.

"It's the waiting," said Torrence to no one and to everyone. "It's the waiting."

The sounds of the firing rose and fell but the distance to the battle was dropping off. Jefferson and the point could hear the sounds clearly now. Rapid firing of machine guns and the slower shooting of rifles and pistols. Once in a while they could hear a shout. A human voice raised in anger or in pain. It meant that someone still survived.

They reached a row of buildings along a street. There was noise from the other side of them, as if the aliens were in the street there. Jefferson held up a hand and stopped the point platoon. Using hand signals, he deployed the soldiers, sending them right and left, but keeping them out on the street.

Then, slowly, they entered the buildings, moving through them. Jefferson hesitated as the soldiers followed his orders. When the street was empty, he pushed on the door closest to him. It swung open quietly, easily, revealing the interior of a house.

Thinking of the living conditions on Earth, with people seeking shelter in stairways, in hallways, and in the lobbies of hotels, the interior of the house was luxurious. Open floor with only two chairs and a single overturned table. It was a parlor

for receiving guests and it explained why men and women
braved the dangers of spacetravel and unknown worlds. It got
them out of the poverty and the feeling of helplessness on
Earth. It gave them a chance at a good life.

He moved to the rear of the building and found a set of stairs
that led up to the second floor. Taking them two at a time, he
reached the landing and moved down a narrow hallway not
quite believing that all the space could belong to one family. It
seemed almost decadent.

At the rear, he pushed into a bedroom. There was a narrow
cot against one wall, a chest on the other, and a desk on the
third. Over the desk was a window. Ducking, Jefferson moved
to the window and peeked out. He was overlooking another
street, this one filled with the aliens.

Dropping back, he wasn't sure what to do. There were more
than a hundred of the creatures below him. Climbing back to
his feet, he looked out again. All of them were armed and they
were moving forward slowly like the line in front of a store that
announced it had fresh fruit. A long, thick line, as the people
waited for a chance to get in.

He made his way out the door and down the hallway. At the
stairs he hesitated and then hurried down them. Outside, he
saw that the company was coming up the street. Using hand
signals, he directed the soldiers to fan out along the street.
Passing the word along the line, he told them to get to the rear
of the buildings and hold their fire. They were not to shoot until
he opened fire. Then everyone was to pour everything they had
down into the street killing everything that moved.

With two enlisted soldiers, Jefferson ran back into the
building. Whispering, he told them, "We've got good positions at the window in the back of the house."

Together they ran up the steps. Jefferson pointed into one
room and then entered the other. The woman was with him. He
motioned her low and they crawled to the window, one on each
side of it.

"I'll fire first," he said. "A burst through the glass. Then
you hit them from your side. We'll trade off."

"Yes, sir."

Jefferson slipped back and checked his weapon. Then for a
moment he was frozen in time. His mind was back on another

planet where he was a young lieutenant and his sergeant was telling him he'd better do something. He was the young lieutenant afraid to act, afraid to move until the sergeant had taken charge and crawled out to gain the glory that Jefferson now basked in. The sergeant had done it all and he had done nothing. Here was a chance to redeem himself, at least partially.

He glanced at the woman. A young woman with black hair and black eyebrows and dark eyes. She was a beautiful woman who should have been somewhere else using her beauty. Instead she was hunched against a wall, a laser in her hands and sweat soaking her uniform. It was beaded on her upper lip and on her forehead. And her eyes were large and round because she was scared stiff.

That was it, thought Jefferson. Everyone scared stiff. Some do the job and some don't and some die. It was just the way it was. He grinned at her and gave her a short, sharp little nod.

When she grinned in response, Jefferson stood, whirled, and fired out the window. The glass melted in an instant and the beam stabbed out and down, into the mass of alien soldiers. Two or three went down.

As Jefferson dodged to the rear, the woman sprang forward and fired. She swung her weapon back and forth, holding the trigger down as the beam cut through the remainder of the glass and then into the wall around the window.

Then it was Jefferson's turn again. He fired into the street. There were a dozen bodies lying there, but the aliens hadn't figured out the problem. They were still pressing forward. Jefferson shot again and again.

All at once the scene changed. There were high-pitched wails like sirens. Firing erupted from the street. Bullets crashed into the house. Across the street, aliens fired, up at the roofs. They didn't know where the humans were. They shot their weapons as they suddenly tried to get out of the street. Panic rocked through them.

Jefferson stayed in the window shooting. The rest of the company was now in the fighting. Aliens were falling in piles in the street. Their blood flowed thickly, moving into the gutters. There were cries below. Screams of surprise and pain.

The woman joined him then. She knelt down and angled her

shots across the street, sweeping the area with the pale red beam. Aliens tumbled to the pavement. Some tried to squirm to cover. Others lay where they had fallen.

The woman was screaming at the top of her voice and shaking her head. She was lost in the rage of the battle. She wasn't aware of the bullets suddenly snapping around her head. She only saw the creatures below her that had to be killed.

The last attack came as a surprise. There was no opening fire by the machine guns. There was nothing except the quiet surge of the aliens as they poured into the streets and rushed the barricade. They boiled up the street, firing their weapons as soon as they had a target.

Reardon rose up to meet the threat. He aimed his laser and pulled the trigger, but nothing happened. He looked down at it and realized that the power pack was exhausted. Too much firing too fast. No chance for the charge to rebuild and no chance to recharge it.

Tossing it aside, he ducked and scrambled to the right. There he found a rifle dropped by a wounded human. Back in business, he slipped forward, bracing his foot on the rubble and lifting himself higher. Out of the corner of his eye he saw Rachel take his old position and begin shooting at the aliens.

"Get them, girl!" he shouted and then was up, shooting too. Single shots, spaced as he tried to kill the aliens.

This attack didn't seem to have the fire of the last ones. It was a halfhearted attempt to get to the humans. The firing wasn't as intense and there was no machine-gun support.

Reardon climbed higher. He sat back, leaning against the side of a box, bracing himself there. He aimed his rifle, fired, and aimed again. One alien went down but the second round missed. The aliens turned their attention to him, shooting at him. Bullets smashed into the debris kicking up splinters and chips. Reardon ducked but didn't move. He kept firing.

The bullets kept striking the barricade near him. A stone clipped him near the eye. It was a brief, flaring pain. He clapped his hand to his face and found it covered in blood. There was a sudden, second pain, high in his chest. Without knowing it, Reardon slipped from his perch. He tumbled to the street and lay there on his side, unaware of what was happening around him. The street was growing dark and he wondered if they had fought through the day.

Rachel saw him fall and abandoned her position. She reached him as he was trying to sit up. She took his hand and said, "Be still. I'll get help."

"I'm fine," he said but then found he couldn't move. Glancing at her, he added, "It's getting dark."

She looked toward the sun still high in the sky but she didn't contradict him. "Dark," she said.

And then, before he could say anything more, he coughed up a splash of bright red blood. Looking as if he'd just vomited on a host's new carpet, he said, "Sorry." That was the last word he spoke.

The battle suddenly shifted. At first the aliens had been trying to get in toward the center of the city but suddenly that was no longer important to them. The rush shifted just as a tide sometimes did. First one direction and then, suddenly, another. The aliens turned and tried to get out of the city.

Jefferson moved closer to the window and continued to fire down into the street. Now he could see the rest of the company there, also shooting. The aliens were dying quickly. But that didn't stop them. They kept running, trying to get out.

As soon as the flow had ceased near him, Jefferson turned and ran from the room. He flew down the steps and hit the front door. He hesitated there, making sure that none of the enemy was in the street, and then exited the building. Running along the sidewalk, he was yelling at the soldiers, trying to get them out. Now was the time to follow up the advantage. Press the attack because the enemy was in flight.

The soldiers were soon pouring out of the buildings. Jefferson turned then and ran up a cross street, coming out behind where the aliens had been. Waiting for the company to join him, he scanned the street. Nothing. The aliens were gone.

When the soldiers fell in behind him, he waved them forward. The attack, with the leading element twenty soldiers across, rushed up the street, leaping the bodies of the dead aliens. There was an occasional shot as one of the soldiers killed a wounded alien.

They raced up the street trying to catch the fleeing aliens.

Firing erupted in front of them and they slowed so that they wouldn't get killed by their own people. But as they reached the new battle site, the fighting was over and the aliens running in a different direction.

Jefferson walked out toward the company commander. There were fifty or sixty dead aliens in front of his position. Jefferson pointed at them and said, "Well done, Captain."

"That's got it covered," he said. "We got most of them. Stragglers are trying to get out."

Jefferson suddenly realized that the sounds of the fighting had tapered all around him. Smoke still hung heavy and they had yet to contact the civilian defenders, but part of the fighting was over. That was obvious.

And then the final proof came. One of the commo people approached. "Colonel, I have contact with the fleet."

Jefferson looked at the woman, grinned, and said, "Then order them to get the rest of the regiment down here."

"Yes, sir." The woman moved off to transmit the orders.

"Now what, Colonel?"

"We rally and then move toward the center of the city to provide them with assistance." Grinning broadly, he added quickly, "And then we can go home."

21

"SHIP APPROACHING FROM the starboard, Captain," said Jenkins.

"A single ship?"

"Aye, sir. Appears by size and configuration to be one of the two vessels that fled earlier."

"Communications open?"

"Yes, sir."

"What are you going to do?" asked Torrence.

Clemens glanced at her but didn't answer the question. Instead he turned his attention to the screen. The lone ship hung off behind them making no move to close the distance or to try to escape.

"Do we fire, Captain?"

"Negative. They have yet to make a hostile move. Target them but do not fire."

"Aye aye."

"Captain," said Jenkins, "jamming has ceased."

Torrence felt her stomach grow cold. She glanced at the screen but saw only the enemy ship in the distance. "Contact with the ground," she said, her voice shaking.

"Nothing important," said Jenkins. "We've got contact established with the landing force."

"Thank God," said Torrence. "Can you put me through to Colonel Jefferson."

"Negative."

"Why?"

"Major," snapped Clemens, "please remember that you are on my bridge."

She was going to shout back but remembered her military training. She said, "Yes, sir."

"Ship's advancing on us," said Jenkins.

"Targeting?"

"We have him covered. Awaiting your orders, Captain."

"Jenkins, are you picking up anything from that ship?"

"No, sir. No response to our friendship message or to our inquiries. Scanners report that the ship is inhabited and that its defensive systems are armed and ready."

Clemens turned and looked at the screen. He watched as the enemy vessel paralleled his course. It was the same tactic taken when there had been three ships.

"Captain, are we going to wait for the attack?"

Clemens studied the picture. The ship was half the size of his own. His fleet had a number of large combat vessels. The enemy ship posed no real threat, except that it was out there. Clemens could think of no reason to give them the first shot. Doing so could endanger the lives of his sailors and Jefferson's soldiers.

"Targeting, if we do not receive a response to our messages in thirty seconds, I want you to disable that craft."

"Aye, sir."

Clemens leaned to the side and touched a button on the arm of his chair. "Major Beal."

A moment later a voice said, "Beal here."

"Major Beal, have your Marines standing by for a boarding party."

"Aye, sir. We'll move down to the docking bay now. Beal out."

"You're not going to try to board that ship, are you?" asked Torrence.

"Of course," said Clemens.

"Sir," said Jenkins, "they're turning their side toward us. I think they're going to fire."

"Targeting. Take them."

"Firing, sir."

There wasn't much to see on the screen. The enemy ship stopped suddenly and light burst along one of its sides. There was a flare out into space that faded rapidly. The ship did not begin to move again.

"Helm, move us in toward that ship."

"Aye, Captain."

Clemens again touched the button. "Are you ready, Major Beal."

"Aye, sir. I have a company standing by in the docking bay."

"Helm, let's put our docking bay against their main hatch. Targeting, keep them under the guns. Jenkins, you monitor their communications frequencies."

The ship on the screen loomed larger as they approached it. There was no attempt by the ship to flee and there was no return fire from it. It drifted there like a dead hulk waiting for the salvage teams to retrieve it.

"Life support functional?" asked Clemens.

"Aye, sir," said Jenkins. "I have sensor readings indicating that there are survivors on board."

Again Clemens leaned to the side. "Major Beal, we are approaching the enemy vessel. I have been advised that there are survivors on board."

"Understand survivors."

Clemens sat up and watched as the ship grew until it filled the screen and then slipped away, out of sight. Jenkins punched a button and the ship reappeared, directly under their ship. There was a moment when it seemed that both ships were frozen in space and then a sudden clank that reverberated through the ship.

"Docking complete," said Jenkins unnecessarily.

"Go, Major Beal," ordered Clemens.

There was a moment's hesitation and then Beal came up on the commo. "Hatch's open. We're going to board the ship."

Clemens wiped the sweat from his face. He stood up and then sat right back down.

"First troops into the enemy ship," said Beal.

Clemens nodded but didn't say a word.

"Scanners show the enemy forces at the far end of the ship. Integrity was breached near midships," said Jenkins.

Clemens touched the button. "You monitor that, Major."

"Yes, sir."

There was silence for a moment and then Beal came back on. "We've penetrated the interior of the ship. Instrumentation is labeled in old Earth languages."

"What?" said Jenkins out loud but not over the commo.

Beal added. "Looks to be French. Alphabet is the same as ours."

"Earth ship," said Clemens. "Jenkins, get intelligence up here now."

"Aye, sir."

It was then quiet on the bridge except for the sounds of the sensors and the scanners. No one spoke. Their eyes were fixed on the screen that showed nothing other than the black mass of the enemy ship. No one dared to breathe. No one dared to speak.

Then, suddenly, Beal's voice cut through. "We have found bodies. They are human. I repeat. They are human."

"Shit," said Clemens. "I don't like that."

The doors of the elevator opened and Carter stepped out. "You wanted me, Captain?"

"You'll do. Major Beal and our boarding party report that the ships we engaged are from Earth."

Carter nodded and said simply, "Yes, sir."

"No comments?"

"None, sir. Makes some sense."

"I don't see that," said Clemens. "Makes no sense to me. Earth people attacking us." He ignored the discussions they had earlier about the Euro-Africa Economic Block.

The commo crackled and Beal reported, "We have reached an area that is barricaded. Hatches are locked."

"Break through."

"Aye, sir."

Carter looked at the black screen. He glanced over at Torrence and then asked, "Should I remain?"

"Stay where you are," said Clemens.

Those were the last words spoken on the bridge for five minutes. Over the commo, they could hear the breathing of the soldiers on the enemy ship. There were quiet comments among the soldiers as they worked to break through the locked hatches. Beal gave orders, first bringing forward one of the large lasers and then positioning his soldiers for the attack once the hatch was broken.

"Ready to move, Captain," said Beal.

"Go."

"Burn it," said Beal. "Go! Go! Go!"

There was a moment of silence and then, "They've surrendered, Captain."

"Are any of the officers alive?"

"Third officer is here, sir."

"Leave your men to guard the prisoners and bring the officer to the bridge."

"Aye, sir."

Torrence spoke up then. "Can we contact the ground. I need to confer with Colonel Jefferson."

Clemens nodded. "Set up the down-link."

Torrence moved across the bridge and stood behind Jenkins as she worked. Finally the communications officer said, "Link established."

Jefferson didn't wait for more communications with the ships. There was nothing there that he wanted to hear. It was now important to move toward the center of the city and relieve the people there. He was aware of the second shuttle lifts coming down. He heard them as they flew over bringing in more of the regiment. He also knew that those later arrivals had made contact with the enemy, but it was incidental. The aliens fled at the first shots. They were no longer interested in engaging the human forces.

With three companies of the First Battalion, Jefferson again began moving through the streets. This time they moved slowly, checking the buildings around them. Flankers and points were out. Men and women were also moving along the tops of the buildings, making sure that they were clear. Reports indicated that they were finding evidence of an alien presence. Abandoned equipment was strewn on the tops, much of it had been manufactured on Earth, though all of it bore labeling of European countries.

They kept moving, leaving a few people as a rear guard as they penetrated deeper into the city. Finally they came to an area with hundreds of alien bodies. They were piled high in places. Ripped, broken bodies, some of them cut apart by laser blasts and others torn apart by rifle fire. Jefferson realized they had reached the edge of the battleground where the real fighting had taken place.

He halted the command and called the officers together. To them he said, "I'll advance with a small group of people. Everyone else follow at fifty yards. Everyone move slowly. We don't want any of our people killed by a trigger-happy defender. Any questions?"

There were none.

The advance party stuck close to the cover for a few minutes more. Then in the distance they could see one of the barricades erected across the street. More alien bodies, piled three and four high in some places, lay scattered in front of the barricade.

"No movement," said one of the scouts.

"Let's just press on," said Jefferson. He held his weapon in both hands at port arms. He hadn't left the weapon behind because the people at the barricade wouldn't confuse his patrol for another alien attack.

Now they moved to the center of the street so that humans wouldn't be confused by shadows. They fanned out, spreading across the street, and began to walk toward the barricade.

As they approached, Jefferson shouted, "Behind the barricade. Defenders behind the barricade. We're coming in."

There was no immediate response. Then a single head popped up over the top of the barricade. It disappeared quickly and then there was a shout. A scream of joy and suddenly the barricade was swarming with people. Shouting, screaming, laughing people.

Jefferson held up a hand to stop his patrol. They stood their ground looking like soldiers about to be overrun by an attacking horde. In seconds they were surrounded by the people demanding to know who they were and why it took them so long to get there.

Jefferson separated himself from a woman who was clinging to him like he was the last man in the universe. Holding her at arm's length, he asked, "Who's in charge here?"

She grinned and pointed toward a short, stocky man. "Terry Jackson's in charge."

"Thanks." Jefferson moved toward the man and said, "Terry Jackson, I'm Colonel David Jefferson."

The man turned and asked, "Where in the hell have you been?"

Jefferson shrugged and said, "We're here now. What's your status?"

"We've had to abandon most of the city. Survivors of the various outposts are straggling in. Colony is in shambles and I don't know if we can ever put it back together."

"Is there someplace else we can talk?" Jefferson had to raise his voice to be heard above the shouting of the people surrounding him and his tiny band.

The man grinned broadly and then waved a hand at one of the abandoned buildings. Together the two men forced their way through the crowd and then inside. They stopped just inside the door.

"Mr. Jackson, just what is your situation here?"

"Now that you've arrived, much improved. We were able to repulse attacks by the aliens earlier. Most of the people are protected in the center here. I've got a perimeter established."

"Food and supplies?" asked Jefferson.

"Adequate. We had to abandon, or maybe I should say some of our outposts had to abandon fields, but we can move back to harvest the crops. Warehouses are full and there is plenty of edible game in the hills. The bay is full of fish."

The cheering from outside was increasing. Jackson glanced at the window. "Word is spreading," he said. He then turned his attention back to Jefferson. "What made the aliens turn hostile all of a sudden?"

"You didn't initiate the conflict?"

"Hell, Colonel, why would we do that? Plenty of space all around for everyone. We're established on this one continent but not any of the other twelve. There are barely fifty thousand . . . or were barely fifty thousand of us here. We had almost no contact with the aliens. I don't know what happened."

Jefferson nodded. "Well, it's over now."

"Then we can get back to work," said Jackson. "This war has cost us a lot of progress."

"You plan to stay?"

"Hell, Colonel, why would we want to leave?"

Through the broken window he could see the bodies of the dead spread in the street. He thought of the abandoned camps that he had seen with the humans lying dead all around. But then he remembered what it had looked like on the Earth. Thousands of people fighting over a small square of ground or floor so that they would have a place to sleep the night. People dying for that and in the morning they didn't own the space. If someone stronger or smarter came along, they lost it.

And the day was a struggle to survive. The air was filthy, looking yellowish. Food was scarce and what there was of it wasn't always edible. Life was a fight. Life was short and the opportunities were limited.

In comparison, this planet was a paradise. More land than anyone could use, air that was fresh and clean, and food roaming everywhere. For those on Earth with an adventurous spirit, an escape could be found, but where would these people go. What could be better than what they had here?

Jefferson looked at Jackson and said, "I haven't the faintest idea why you'd want to leave."

"We live in paradise," said Jackson.

"We can stay on station here until we learn what happened. We can offer protection and assistance."

"Thank you, Colonel. We can offer the perfect place for leave. Hospitality."

"We'll work out the details later." There was a new burst of noise as more people joined the celebration. Looking through the window again, Jefferson said, "We'd better hold down the parties until we have a few things worked out."

"I hate being the level-headed one with the responsibility," said Jackson. "Sometimes I would just like to lose myself in the party."

"It's the price of command," said Jefferson.

"And sometimes I don't think it's worth it."

Together they moved back into the street.

22

THE REGIMENT HAD been rejoined and the garrison had been established on the outskirts of the city. Patrols ranged out from there, toward the old human outposts, but the alien threat had vanished with the destruction of the French ships in space. The capture, or rather the surrender, of the last of those ships had ended the alien desire to fight.

To prepare his final report, Jefferson called his staff officers together in the conference room. Clemens, sitting on the bridge, declined to join, sending his second in command. She sat at the table along with Major Beal of the Marines.

Jefferson stood at the head of the table and said, "Looks like the situation below has stabilized with no sign of hostile action in the last two weeks. Now, in preparation of forwarding a report to higher headquarters, I need to have a few things clarified."

He stopped talking and looked at the men and women assembled with him. Good soldiers, every one of them. People he could count on in battle. People who weren't glory hounds out for personal gain, but people well trained and well disciplined. Suddenly he realized just how lucky he was to have them as his staff. He grinned briefly, but didn't say a word about his feelings. Instead he said, "Captain Carter."

The intelligence officer stood and glanced down at the computer terminal in front of him. He read for a moment and then said, "Ships standing in space here were from the Euro-African Economic Block, specifically France. Their presence was not in violation of various international treaties and they were trading with the various indigenous peoples. All quite legal and above board."

"Captain," said Jefferson.

"Yes, sir. At any rate, their appearance here, with a weapons and military equipment shipment, coincides with the outbreak of hostilities. It's our belief that the alien cultures, realizing that the human race was expanding into their zones faster than they expected, were trying to halt or at least inhibit that flow. The opportunity to buy advanced electronics and weapons from the French gave them the equipment to eliminate the human presence."

"Christ," said Jefferson.

Carter ignored him and continued. "With a method of blocking our communications and with weapons that matched those we had, they attacked . . ."

"You mean to tell me," said Jefferson, "that the outbreak of hostilities came about because a traveling salesman came to call on them?"

"Yes, sir."

Torrence spoke up. "Aren't there laws to prevent selling of first order equipment to the aliens?"

"Well, yes, Major, but the problem is that France is not a signatory of that agreement, and besides, the equipment isn't of the first order."

"The jamming equipment was of the first order," said Torrence.

"But it's not covered in the agreement," said Carter. "It comes under the heading of communications gear and not weapons. Therefore it was a legal sale."

Jefferson slammed his hand down on the table. "You're splitting hairs."

"No, sir. Not me. It's the way the trade agreements are written. You'll notice that the aliens had few lasers and those they had were not of the quality and reliability of our weapons. Their slug throwers, however, are of the finest available. Fire arms are not covered but lasers are. Politicians designed the agreements."

"Have you talked to the crew of the French ship?"

"Oh, yes, sir," said Carter. He punched at the keyboard of the computer. "They expressed their horror that their equipment was used in a war."

"What in the hell did they think the fire arms were going to be used for?" asked Torrence.

"They didn't say but did say that if they hadn't sold the equipment here, someone else would have."

"The universal cop out," said Jefferson. "My crimes are forgiven because someone would have done it if I hadn't. Bullshit."

Torrence shook her head. "So the aliens attacked our outposts because they thought they could push us off planet and they believed that because they had bought weapons and equipment from us. Well, not us exactly."

"That's about it, Major."

"That has to be one of the dumbest reasons to start a war that I ever heard."

Now Carter shrugged. "Wars on Earth were started for reasons that are equally obscure and equally ridiculous."

Jefferson rocked back in his chair and shook his head. It was too unbelievable to have happened. "I want a formal report drawn up and forwarded to Earth on the first courier."

"Yes, sir," said Torrence. She sat quietly for a moment and then asked, "You think it'll do any good?"

Jefferson spun the chair around and sat down so that he was facing the bulkhead. Finally he turned and put his elbows on the table. "No. But it'll make me feel better." He looked up at Carter. "Anything else?"

"I could go into a complete order of battle, established now that we've pretty well eliminated the enemy."

"File it," said Jefferson. He sat there for a moment and let everything that he had just learned sink in. He let the reasons for the war sink in. No real reason except that the Europeans were there selling their goods to the aliens who saw it as a method of eliminating the human presence on the planet. And the French saw it as a way of opening up more space to their expansion, though there was so much space on the planet that there was no reason to deny immigration to anyone.

Jefferson shook his head. "I think I've heard enough. Captain Carter, work with Major Torrence and prepare the whole report. Now, any questions?"

A figure stood up and then said, "Colonel, you've been avoiding me."

Jefferson laughed. "Wrong, Mr. Garvey. Had I been avoiding you, I wouldn't have allowed you to attend the meeting."

"Yes, well. I'm going to report that your cooperation has been less than sterling."

"You may do anything you want," said Jefferson. He sat quietly for a moment and could almost hear Sergeant Mason telling him to wait. Telling him that timing was everything. When it seemed that he would say nothing more, he added, "But, if you do that, then I will not cooperate with you at all."

"The situation now."

"Nope," said Jefferson. "Just seems that way. But right now I have no reason to deny you access to my communications facilities, my galleys, or my recreational areas."

Garvey stood for a moment and then said, "That sounds like a threat."

"Most perceptive."

"It won't work. I have a job to do."

Jefferson nodded and said, "You cooperate with me and I'll see to it that you're allowed a wider latitude in doing your job. I promise you that."

Garvey, seeing that he could do nothing else, nodded. "Thank you, Colonel."

Jefferson sat there for a moment looking into the faces of his combat staff. Seeing that they wanted to get out of the meeting, he said, "If there is nothing else."

The officers bolted from the conference room. They disappeared through the hatch in seconds, leaving him alone with Torrence.

"Major."

"Colonel."

"Something on your mind?"

Torrence sat quietly for a moment and then asked, "Where's young Lieutenant Norris?"

"Checking out her supplies. Retrieval of the battalion used in the sweep has given her quite a bit of work to do."

"Then we won't be interrupted."

"Only if we stay here."

Torrence rolled her eyes. "Who said anything about staying here?"

Jefferson understood immediately. "Then let's get going."

"I thought you'd never ask."

HIGH-TECH ADVENTURES BY BESTSELLING AUTHORS

____**DAY OF THE CHEETAH**
Dale Brown 0-425-12043-0/$5.50

In Dale Brown's newest *New York Times* bestseller, Lieutenant Colonel Patrick McClanahan's plane, the Cheetah, must begin the greatest high-tech chase of all time.

____**AMBUSH AT OSIRAK**
Herbert Crowder 0-515-09932-5/$4.50

Israel is poised to attack the Iraqi nuclear production plant at Osirak. But the Soviets have supplied Iraq with the ultimate super-weapon . . . and the means to wage nuclear war.

____**ROLLING THUNDER**
Mark Berent 0-515-10190-7/$4.95

The best of the Air Force face the challenge of Vietnam in "a taut, exciting tale . . . Berent is the real thing!"—Tom Clancy

____**FLIGHT OF THE OLD DOG**
Dale Brown 0-425-10893-7/$5.50

The unthinkable has happened: The Soviets have mastered Star Wars technology. And when its killer laser is directed across the globe, America's only hope is a battle-scarred bomber—the Old Dog Zero One.
